A TOASTER ON MARS

DARRELL PITT

TEXT PUBLISHING MELBOURNE AUSTRALIA

textpublishing.com.au

The Text Publishing Company
Swann House
22 William Street
Melbourne Victoria 3000
Australia

First published in 2016 by The Text Publishing Company

Cover design by Imogen Stubbs
Page design by Text
Typeset by J&M Typesetting

Printed in Australia by Griffin Press, an Accredited ISO AS/NZS 14001:2004 Environmental Management System printer

National Library of Australia Cataloguing-in-Publication entry:
Creator: Pitt, Darrell, author.
Title: A toaster on Mars / by Darrell Pitt.
ISBN: 9781922182869 (paperback)
ISBN: 9781925095760 (ebook)
Subjects: Detective and mystery stories.
Dewey Number: A823.4

To Aimée
As promised

A NOTE FROM THE EDITOR

I'm Zeeb Blatsnart.

Yes, *that* Zeeb Blatsnart. No doubt you know me from my appearances on the Interplanetary Nature Channel—*Prodding Exotic Creatures, The Glecks of Totalis Four* and *The Rhinorats of Sirius*. There are few corners of the galaxy to which I have not travelled, and little I have not seen with my five eyes. Some may consider me a know-it-all, but I prefer to think of myself as being better informed than anyone else in the universe.

I've been asked to edit this adventure about Blake Carter, a law-enforcement agent living on Earth. Oh, you haven't heard of Earth? I'm not surprised. It's a rather polluted blue dot suffering from global warming, overpopulation and not enough people using deodorant.

Some may see my editing of this book as a demotion, but nothing could be further from the truth. It is true: I was recently suspended from the Interplanetary Nature Channel for killing Tosho Twelve's last rhinopig—but there were extenuating circumstances. I hadn't eaten all day! And what would you rather have: a happy celebrity or a live rhinopig?

I will return to the Interplanetary Nature Channel. It's just taking some time to renegotiate my contracts.

Meanwhile, I have chosen to earn a few trifling credits as an editor.

Ah, the trials of life...

First, I should make clear that at no point in this story does a toaster appear on the planet Mars. Nor on Jupiter, Venus, Mercury or any other planet local to Earth. There isn't even a toaster in any nearby star system, although there *is* a waffle maker on Rygil Five and a rather nice casserole dish on Xypod Nine, but these culinary devices have nothing to do with our story.

I should also point out that reading this book prior to the 26th century is breaking the law. The penalty for such a crime is nine years in jail and 300 hours of listening to *The Greatest Hits of Looloo Jones and his Singing Dachshund Quartet*.

So don't blame me if the Time Police come bursting through your door and drag you kicking and screaming into an inter-dimensional black hole.

Oh, and for a limited time only, the first ninety-seven seasons of my program, *The Tarbils of Sataris*, are available as a boxed set. Ring 555-334-455-663-322-441-0107 within sixty seconds to receive a complimentary slice of rhinopig.

Zeeb Blatsnart, Editor

1

'Blake! It's time to get up!'

Groaning, Blake Carter peered at the owl-shaped alarm clock. He hated everything about that clock—its leer, its bright mustard-yellow eyes—but most of all he hated its voice; it sounded too much like his mother.

'You'll be late for work,' the clock said. 'And you know how grumpy that makes you.'

'Shut up,' Blake muttered.

'See what I mean.'

The night before, Blake had drunk not one but eight or nine too many Plutonium Supernovas at the Pink Hyperdrive, his local bar. Afterwards he had still been able to walk, but not in a straight line.

Blake's eyes swept towards the window. His apartment, wedged between two buildings, looked over a narrow slice of Neo City. Last night he'd forgotten to turn on the blind and now he could see space elevators rising into orbit, lines of flying cars, and an advertising blimp flashing on and off.

New at the movies!
Star Trek 159: The Wrath of Khan's Clone!
Starts Friday!

'Just give me a minute,' Blake said.

'You said that five minutes ago,' the alarm said. 'If you don't get up now, I'll have to turn nasty.'

'You don't mean—'

The alarm clock gave a laugh that Blake didn't like. 'I'll sing,' it said. 'And you know what my singing's like.'

This got Blake out of bed. The alarm had once woken him with a version of 'Dancing Queen', sung in Icelandic and badly out of tune. Blake's ears had rung all day.

'In the old days,' he muttered, 'alarms used to buzz or chime.'

'Well, now it's the 26th century,' the clock said, as if Blake were a dodo. 'We live in a more enlightened age.'

'Really?' Blake snatched up a shoe and hurled it at the clock, knocking it off the bookshelf. 'Enlighten that.'

The plastic owl smashed to the floor. 'Now look what you've done!' it wailed. 'You've broken my—'

Whatever Blake had broken would forever remain a mystery as the clock died with a gasp.

Blake lurched across the room and hit the switch for his coffee pot. He wasn't a fan of technology. Once upon a time, people had hunted, gathered, and worn animal skins. It was a system that worked—apart from the small risk of being eaten by sabre-tooth tigers. Everything these days ran on fission power, resembled something it shouldn't and was always looking for an argument.

His attack on the clock had knocked a few books off his shelf. *Real* books. Not plastic or electronic or those Immersion Books where you were part of the story. These were actually made of paper.

Blake's home was four-metres square, with a sonar-shower in one corner and a kitchen nook in another. Blake liked his humble abode, although his ex-wife, Astrid, had once described the style as a cross between early ugly and eternal damnation.

Now that Blake was up, the bed had automatically folded back into the wall, revealing his wardrobe. His clothes were all identical: seven pairs of cobalt blue pants, seven amber-coloured shirts and seven long trench coats. Blake didn't like variety.

A flat-screen television and family vids decorated the other walls. Most of the vids were of happier times with Astrid and their daughter, Lisa—a week at the Lunar Zoo, the holiday on Titan and their day at the Wet'n'Wild park at the bottom of the Mariana Trench.

His heart gave a lurch when he thought of Lisa. She was the one thing Blake missed about his marriage. He still carried a souvenir with him wherever he went—a tube of water from their holiday on the ocean floor. Lisa had bought it for him. On the side was a slogan, *How Deep is Your Love?*

Sighing, Blake caught sight of himself in the mirror. He was ten pounds overweight, his hair was starting to thin and he had deep lines under his eyes. His knees weren't in great shape and his back ached when it got cold.

Nobody lives forever, he thought. *Except maybe Pleck Wilson.*

Zeeb says:

I should point out that there's some debate about whether Pleck Wilson is actually alive. The film and amusement-park mogul died in 2066 and had his head cryogenically frozen. Two hundred years later, advanced technology meant the head could be brought back to life. But after being taken on a day tour of Earth, Wilson asked to be put back into cold storage.

'This sort of horror,' Wilson said, after seeing 23rd-century Earth, 'I don't need.'

'Good morning, Blake.' The television had now flickered to life, having been activated by the percolating of the coffee machine. 'It's another beautiful day!'

'If you say so.'

'Would you like bad news, really bad news, or catastrophically bad news?'

'I'll go with catastrophic,' Blake replied. 'Things can only improve after that.'

The screen flashed to a pair of blue-skinned news anchors. '*Two billion people dead as the Tyrus Five sun unexpectedly goes supernova! Rescue ships are being sent from Tyrus Four to search for survivors.*'

They were trying to look horrified, but it was clear they were barely able to contain their glee at breaking such a huge story.

'They'd better take suncream,' the female anchor joked. 'It's going to be really *toasty* on the surface!'

'Off,' Blake told the television and it sputtered back to silence.

After thirty-eight seconds in the sonar shower, Blake emerged clean, and feeling almost human. A minute later he was dressed.

His wristcomm rang.

'Yeah?'

'Blake Carter?' It was dispatch. 'There's a special briefing at 8am.'

As an agent with the Planetary Bureau of Investigation, Blake was used to receiving calls at all hours. With branches in every city on Earth, the PBI's role was to investigate crimes too big for the local authorities.

Blake frowned. 'But the daily briefing's always at 9am.'

'That's why it's called a *special* briefing.'

'What's it about?'

But dispatch had already disconnected.

Must be something big, Blake thought. *There hasn't been a briefing that early since the assassination of Kennedy's clone.*

On the top ledge of his bookshelf sat his hat—a scarlet fedora. Blake took it down and put it on. He and this hat had been through a lot.

'Don't forget your breakfast,' his refrigerator reminded him. 'It's the most important meal of the day.'

Blake took out a bottle of pink pills. On the side it read *Bacon and Eggs*. He shook two into his hand.

'Watch your weight,' his fridge said.

Rolling his eyes, Blake ate them, grabbed a second bottle and stuffed them into his pocket.

The hallway outside his apartment was a cramped, gloomy corridor shared by a hundred other residents, most of them off-worlders. A family from Baxhill Six—a small marsupial race—shoved past without speaking to Blake. He'd been on their bad side since they first moved in, after chasing them with a chair, thinking they were mutant rats. No amount of apologising had mended the rift.

Some species just aren't forgiving.

The day outside was humid and gloomy, the air thick with smog—but this passed for sunny in Neo City.

Zeeb says:

You know those communities where public transport is efficient, pollution is kept to a minimum and people work together for peace and harmony?

Well, Neo City isn't one of them. It's a multi-layered metropolis with buildings a thousand storeys high, linked by a million walkways and roads. Sunlight permeates the upper levels, but it's artificial light most of the way down, with complete darkness at the bottom. People and 'things' live down there, but mostly the things have the upper hand.

Don't go to the bottom, not even on a dare.

Neo City was built on what used to be the east coast of an obsolete country called the United States. Buried under five centuries of construction is a mouldy green statue of a lady with a torch and a book. There's also a pretty nice building that used to be called the White House—but now it's mostly brown, held together with Wonder-Glue and occupied by a homeless guy named Ernie who lives there with his six-legged rat, Felix.

Blake sighed. He lived on the 701st level, on the east side of town. There were better places to live, but a PBI agent didn't make enough money to live in them.

He joined the crowded footpath. A man passed by wearing a T-shirt with bright words flashing *Don't Buy Stuff!* Following him came a woman walking a pair of Labrador-giraffes, and then a girl zoomed past on a tricycle-copter with a choir of dolls singing Beethoven's 'Ode to Joy' in a basket.

Robots were everywhere. The League of Planets Charter forbade them resembling sentient life forms, including humans, but most were bipedal, with two arms, a torso and head. Many others had one leg, three legs, four legs—or more. Some even glided. They were every colour imaginable and made of plexy-plastic or hydro-metal, and all were equipped with AI brains, their intelligence ranging from that of a goldfish to an Einstein, Hawking or Slugmeyer.

Blake gazed about the street. Advertisements pulsated and gyrated on walls and windows, selling everything from diapers to holidays on the moon. This part of town had every building style imaginable: Art Deco, Greek Aluminium, Romanesque and Platinum Gothic, Rubber Classical, Tin Byzantium. Most of the apartments had small balconies with flowerboxes of balloon azaleas, which were all the rage this year.

Endless lines of flying cars, buses, taxi-gondolas and helium-cyclists moved around the city. Another advertising blimp floated past promoting *Al's Doughnut Burgers: Lo Cal Centres!* Teenagers on skateboards jumped off walkways, dropped a dozen floors and activated rockets to land safely below.

Blake took a deep breath, inhaling something that tasted like a cross between burnt plastic and toffee apple.

Neo City, he thought. *Home, sweet home.*

2

'Must you continue this madness?'

It was the first thing Sally—his red and white replica 1956 Chevrolet Bel Air—said to Blake as he approached.

She was parked in a narrow alley adjacent to the building. Blake had only owned the car for six weeks and she hadn't done anything for his stress levels.

'What madness?' Blake asked as he slid behind the wheel.

Sally's interior was also a replica of the original, except for some additional switches set into the dash. A nuclear fission propulsion system sat under the bonnet.

'This *driving* madness.'

'Everyone drives. That's not crazy at all.'

'No,' Sally said. 'The car does the driving. You should be watching television or cruising the Hypernet.'

'I'm an old-fashioned guy. And what's it to you, anyway?'

'I've a right to be worried about my safety.'

'I'm a good driver.'

'Did you tell that to the other twelve cars, too?'

Blake didn't reply. He *had* said that to his previous cars, but they had still all met unfortunate ends. *Well*, he reasoned. *Thirteen's a lucky number, isn't it?*

'Being a PBI agent is a dangerous job,' he said.

'I worry about you, Blake.'

'You can't worry. You're an AI—an artificial intelligence.'

Blake started the engine and, within seconds, had joined a line of cars. He flew towards PBI headquarters.

Everyone had replica cars these days, but most of them were in better shape than Blake's Bel Air. While most people sat in the driver's seat and read books or surfed the Hypernet, Blake focused on keeping Sally between the floating lane buoys. He liked driving. It made him feel like he was still in control, instead of surrendering to technology.

The early-morning traffic was worse than the Battle of the Bulge, and it took him half an hour to reach headquarters.

Despite having worked there for fifteen years, the view still took Blake's breath away.

Zeeb says:

How do you define big?

Its meaning has long been debated. The universe has been called big, but then my Auntie Dukmaj is big, too—she eats too many doughnuts. So instead of calling Neo City's PBI headquarters big, let's say it's larger than a breadbox and smaller than a Neptunian whale.

Covering twenty-two city blocks, PBI headquarters is the second-largest building in Neo City, dwarfed only by the McBurgers on 34th Street. Here, thousands of agents investigate robberies, kidnappings, murders and—most difficult of all—temporal crimes.

Temporal crimes are when people travel through time to change history. Anyone making an attempt is thrown into jail without a chance of parole.

To put PBI headquarters into context, it's so large that the Missing Persons Bureau was missing for three months before it was found in the basement of the north wing.

Blake parked Sally in the underground car park and headed to the main concourse, which was an enormous dome-shaped chamber. Dozens of PBI agents sat on one side of the bookings desk, patiently trying to determine if crimes needed investigating, ridiculing or ignoring, while the public, queued on the other side of the desk, screamed and cried as they waved paperwork clenched in hands, tentacles or gluggy things. Everyone wanted justice, or their version of it.

Message robots weaved through the crowd, passing beneath the B-class security scanners. A new desk opened for business and one robot was knocked over and trampled in the frenzy to be served.

Blake pushed through the crowd to the security entrance at the far end, pausing at the barriers. The detectors on either side fired x-rays, ultraviolet light, alpha waves and enough energy to power a cloned AC/DC concert. He was amazed anyone survived the experience without glowing in the dark.

He headed to the briefing room on the 300th floor, a huge hall with standing room only. *The last time I saw this many agents was at the last Christmas party*, he thought. *And most of them were drunk or comatose.*

A man pushed through the crowd to a stage at the front.

Sprot! That's Cecil Pomphrey.

The assistant director only left the office for one of three reasons: hard drinking, football and delivering bad news. Blake doubted he was here to share a drink or toss a ball around.

Those who hadn't yet had the pleasure of meeting Cecil Pomphrey always received a shock. The name Cecil tended to conjure up the image of a skinny man with glasses, dressed in a slightly too large suit. A man who, possibly, lived with his elderly mother, watching old movies each night while eating shortbread biscuits and drinking cups of watery tea.

Cecil Pomphrey looked like a wrestler. He was bald, with ears that looked as beaten as a pair of shoes trampled by a herd of Tradian elephants. His hands were so large that more than one subordinate had suggested calling the *Galactic Book of Records* to make a claim. His voice was a growl, as if he spent his spare time gargling lava.

Zeeb says:

Through a strange coincidence, I am actually related by marriage to Cecil Pomphrey. His wife is my third cousin, Barbara, who is twice removed from my Auntie Bluck. Although that information has no bearing on this story, it's interesting how we're all related to each other, and yet another reason why we should have intergalactic peace.

'PBI agents,' Pomphrey's booming voice cut through the chatter of the assembled throng, 'thank you for your prompt attendance.'

The room fell silent.

'At 10pm last night, a weapon of unimaginable destruction was stolen from the Ministry of Defence. It was a Super-EMP device—the most powerful ever developed.'

An agent near Blake frowned. 'What's a Super-EMP?' he asked.

'It can wipe out all electrical devices on Earth,' Blake

explained. 'Hospitals, transportation, water recycling, food distribution—they'd all fail. Billions of lives would be lost, plunging Earth into a new Dark Age.'

'What about television?'

'There would be no television.'

'No television,' the agent muttered. 'That's serious.'

A loud buzz had broken out. Pomphrey held up his hands for quiet.

'The perpetrator of the crime has demanded a ransom of 100 billion credits. If the money is not paid within five days to an off-planet account, he'll use the weapon.'

Another agent held up her hand. 'You're saying *he*,' she said. 'Do you know who's responsible?'

'The perpetrator is Bartholomew Badde,' Pomphrey said, his eyes sweeping the room to eventually settle on Blake.

Bartholomew Badde.

Blake's vision swam. The criminal mastermind was famous throughout the galaxy and aspired to be remembered as history's greatest villain.

Badde had evaded the law for so many years that most departments had given up on trying to catch him— he had changed his face more than a dozen times so that no one now knew what he looked like. The assignment had been handed over to Blake and his partner, Bailey Jones. Following Badde to Venus, they had been crossing a volcanic plain when—

Blake shook his head. The memory was too painful.

Pomphrey had started talking again. 'One of our agents has been following up on Badde for years,' he said, 'and his research will be distributed shortly. This will be our number one priority until this crisis is over. Badde must be stopped.'

Blake caught sight of his section commander, Senior Agent Capelli, who had come marching over. She was Tyrinian, a reptilian race: short and thickset with a cobra-like face and flared neck.

'Looks like you're the man of the hour,' Capelli said.

'Looks like it.'

Capelli took Blake down to her office on the 221st floor. It was a small room with a billboard outside the window flashing *Holidays to Neptune—Bring your woollies!*

Blake had always liked Capelli. She was a no-nonsense agent with a good arrest record. Her wall was decorated with citations for meritorious conduct. She had won Agent of the Year three years running.

Capelli stopped at her desk, reached in and pulled out a snack box. She caught the rat as it leapt out.

'I suppose you still want me heading up the Badde investigation,' Blake said, trying to ignore the squirming rodent. 'I've got some ideas about how to find him.'

'That's great,' she said, biting off the rat's head and wolfing it down. 'We'll need all the help we can get.' She tossed the rest of the rat into her mouth and swallowed.

Blake leant forward. 'What do you mean?'

'Just that—it'll be a team effort.'

'But surely you want me in charge? I'm the expert on Badde.'

Capelli sighed. 'We appreciate the work you've done, Blake,' she said. 'But this is straight from Pomphrey: I'll be taking over from here.'

'I don't understand.'

'We need a team player heading up this investigation,' Capelli said. She took out another rat, which gave Blake a desperate look before it disappeared into Capelli's mouth. 'And you're the only agent in the PBI who works alone.'

'I work better alone.'

'We've taken the liberty of transferring your files to the server.'

'But those are my private files!'

'This is the PBI,' she said, her steely eyes fixing on Blake. 'Nothing's private here.'

Woodenly, Blake made his way to the door. 'I should be heading up this investigation,' he said. 'I know how Badde thinks. I'm the only one who can catch him.'

Capelli put down her snack box and scowled. 'It's that sort of thinking that's kept you off this case,' she said.

Making his way to the lift, Blake checked the main server on his wristcomm.

Sprot!

Capelli had been right: his files had now been shared with the entire bureau. A few passing agents gave him a brief nod. Blake could read their expressions: they knew the case had been taken away from him.

When the lift arrived, he hit the button for the basement. He should have headed for his office, but Capelli's news, not to mention her breakfast, had left his stomach churning.

I need to get out of here, he thought. *I'm the laughing stock of the PBI.*

'Back already?' Sally asked as he climbed behind the wheel. 'Bad day at the office?'

'Quiet,' Blake fumed. On a hunch, he checked his wristcomm again, but this time scanned the mail files. An anonymous message had been delivered to him: *Check the personnel files of the Tygonian temple if you want to locate Bartholomew Badde.*

He tried tracing the message, but it was masked. This could be something or nothing at all. It might be a hoax—but why send him to a Tygonian temple?

'Where are we going?' Sally asked.

Blake started the engine. 'We're going to find God,' he replied.

3

An acid rain fell across Neo City.

It fell on the good, the bad and the ugly, but it especially fell on those who had not bothered to catch the warning on the evening news. It cascaded over the super skyscrapers, down into the deep canyon streets and onto Blake Carter, who was unsuccessfully trying to huddle under an awning.

Short-term exposure was harmless, but any longer could turn a human to sludge. And while Blake did not fear death, he did have an aversion to ending up as anything that didn't look much like him.

Tightening his trench coat, he tipped his scarlet fedora forwards. It was almost 11pm and it had been a long day. It had taken him ages to find a way into the Tygonian temple.

Where is this guy? Blake wondered.

A drunk in a nearby apartment started singing 'Loving My Three-Eyed Girl on Venus'. Mid-chorus, he broke into a loud sob and hurled a chair through his window. Blake watched it bounce down the alley, stunning a pigeon who then crash-landed on a window ledge. The pigeon flapped its wings once before being gobbled up by a carnivorous potted plant on the next ledge.

Blake wrinkled his nose. *What is that smell?*

Looking down, he saw a plastic dog excreting a pile of silicon poo at his feet. The animal gave him a satisfied look before trotting down the alley.

Blake shuffled into the next doorway.

This part of town was about as safe as landing a paper glider on the surface of the sun. PBI agents had come down here and never been seen again.

At least I've got my blaster, he thought.

A monitor next to Blake's face flickered to life. Grey static dissolved into a grinning face.

'Bob Flatulent,' the face introduced itself. 'From Flatulent Insurance. And you are?'

'Nobody,' Blake said.

'Life is unexpected, my friend—'

'Are you selling life insurance?'

'Not at all. I'm offering you an opportunity. Do you know how many people were impaled by musical instruments last year? Twenty-three! I know what you're thinking. A flute, a violin—those you can walk away from. But what about an oboe? A tuba? A trombone? You don't walk away after being impaled by a trombone.'

Blake elbowed the screen and it went dark.

'Salesmen,' he muttered.

A shape moved at the other end of the alley. Checking the blaster under his coat, Blake watched as a man wearing a monk's habit flitted from shadow to shadow until he reached a doorway with the letter 'T' spray-painted over it.

The monk motioned for Blake to approach, pushing back his hood to reveal a goatee, a shaved head and an advertisement on his forehead that read *Joe's Facelifts: You age 'em! We stretch 'em!*

'Brother Puttlik?' Blake said.

'And you are?'

'Blake Carter. Planetary Bureau of Investigation.'

'And you wish to enter the temple? Why?'

'That's PBI business.'

'If it is because of food hygiene, I assure you those grasshoppers were entirely accidental—'

'This has nothing to do with grasshoppers,' Blake said, lowering his voice. 'It's got to do with Bartholomew Badde.'

'The criminal?'

The news had broken during the day about Badde's theft of the Super-EMP. There must have been a leak within the PBI—not surprising considering the significance of the story. The Hypernet had exploded with rumours about the end of civilisation. The stock market had bottomed out. People were scrambling to get off-planet.

The world president had promised the weapon would be recovered. He didn't say if that meant paying Badde or capturing him.

'The entire PBI's trying to track down Badde,' Blake said, 'but it's like looking for a Rastarian needle in a Cytonian haystack.'

Zeeb says:
    Which is really hard, if you didn't already know.

Blake told Puttlik about the tip-off. 'I need to check your personnel files,' he said.

'Access to our computer system is forbidden,' Puttlik said. 'And my faith is strong—'

'How about a hundred credits?'

'—but my wallet is empty.'

Puttlik pulled out a card reader and swiped Blake's cash card. After unlocking the door, he led Blake into a laundry where, from the bottom shelf, he produced a robe, sending a batch of electric cockroaches scurrying.

He handed the robe to Blake. 'Wear this,' he said.

Donning the robe, Blake followed Puttlik into a hall that looked like it had once been an ugly warehouse and had now been transformed into an ugly warehouse *with drapes*.

A fifty-foot cross-legged plastic statue of Tygon had been placed in the centre of the floor. The god looked quite serene, with one hand gently touching a huge wart on his chin as if he were considering the infinite mysteries of the universe. Around him, one hundred devotees meditated, mimicking the pose.

'Impressive,' Puttlik said. 'Yes?'

'Oh,' Blake said. 'Very.'

Zeeb says:

If you're wondering how Tygon gained a following, the answer lies in Garlek's Law, which states that no matter how stupid an idea, there will always be people who will believe it.

In this instance, Tygon, a banker living on Hydor Seven, was fixing his TV antenna during a storm when he fell off his roof, knocking himself unconscious. On waking, he became convinced that God was speaking to him through his wart.

Yes, you read that right. His wart.

For the next thirty years Tygon listened to his wart, carefully jotting down its sage wisdom. If you think a faith based on listening to a talking wart is silly, then I will remind you that Tygonianism is only one of the universe's 12,245,543 major religions. Many are even sillier.

Puttlik silently led Blake past the worshippers and down a winding torch-lit staircase.

'You don't have electricity?' Blake asked.

'It's cosier this way.'

How do I end up in these situations? Blake wondered.

Last month he had faced down a mutant chihuahua, a killer known as the Tickle Torturer, and a car wash that had taken three vehicles hostage, threatening to kill them if the quality of its detergent wasn't improved.

Now this.

After descending a further fifteen flights of stairs, they finally reached the dingy basement. Smelling of mould and mushrooms, the room held another statue of Tygon, this time positioned on a square pedestal.

'We're a long way down,' Blake said, peering into the gloom. 'Is there another way out?'

'Oh, there's the elevator.'

'There's an elevator?'

'But the scenic route is much more interesting.'

Blake resisted the urge to mash Puttlik's face into the wall.

'Where's the mainframe?' he asked instead.

Striding past the statue, Puttlik led Blake to another room where an ancient computer sat on a desk in the corner. Blake attached a hack drive to the system. It took 0.452 seconds to search more than ten billion records.

'Nothing,' he sighed.

'Who is this man?' an angry voice demanded.

Swinging around, Blake saw two devotees in the doorway.

'I don't know,' Puttlik said, wringing his hands. 'I heard a sound and came in to investigate—and here he was!'

'Death is the penalty for breaking into our computer system!' one of the men snapped.

Blake flashed his ID. 'I'm a PBI agent. If anything happens to me, the government will turn your temple into toast—'

'There will be no toasting our temple!'

'—so you'll step aside so I can walk right out of here.'

But one of the men leapt at Blake, grabbing his throat. 'You will not leave here! You will languish in our deepest cell until the end of recorded time! Your only sustenance will be the sweat of the other prisoners—'

Pulling out his blaster, Blake stunned the two men and they collapsed in an untidy heap.

'Where's the elevator?'

'Behind the statue,' Puttlik whimpered. 'But the other devotees will kill me if they think I betrayed them.'

'I don't want that.'

'Neither do I.'

So Blake stunned him too.

'The things I do for love,' he muttered.

Blake realised this could turn very nasty, very quickly. More devotees could turn up at any moment. As the elevator ascended, he sent an emergency signal on his wristcomm. Backup would be here in minutes, but it might be too late.

The doors opened. The prayer session had just ended and devotees were everywhere. Blake pushed through, keeping his head low. He was almost out. Only a few more feet…

'Stop him!' someone yelled. 'He's an infidel!'

Oh, sprot.

Blake waved his badge, firing his blaster into the ceiling, but there were too many of them, and they were picking things up to use as weapons: spoons, mops, books. Someone waved a chainsaw. The door was only a few feet away, but it might as well have been the other side of the galaxy.

'I'm a PBI agent!' he shouted. 'You're all under arrest for assaulting a police officer—' He hit the emergency communicator on his wrist again, but he knew reinforcements wouldn't reach him in time.

A figure appeared waving a trombone.

Sprot!

The musical instrument slammed into Blake's head and everything went black.

4

At first there was darkness. Then a bright spot of light appeared. Blake thought he might have been witnessing the Big Bang—until he realised it was too late for that.

A ceiling shifted into view. *No, this is definitely not the Big Bang.* The Big Bang didn't have a ceiling. Walls arrived. Then windows.

This was a hospital. His eyes shifted to a chair and a man sitting in it.

Sprot, he thought. *Cecil Pomphrey.*

Blake forced himself to sit up. 'Assistant Director,' he said.

Speaking hurt. In fact, *everything* did. He was in more pain now than when he'd fallen into an Inverse

Quantum Polaric Hypersingularity Generator—and that had hurt *a lot*.

'Agent Carter.' Pomphrey's voice was deep. 'You look like crap.'

'Really? Don't hold back…'

'I've seen agents busted up before, but you had bones broken that the docs didn't even know existed.' Pomphrey stood up and began pacing the room. 'I've been watching you, Blake.'

Blake didn't know whether to feel flattered or worried.

'I like to know what's happening with our agents,' Pomphrey continued. 'You used to be one of our top people.'

'Still am,' Blake said. 'I might not be as fast as I once was—'

'I'm not talking about speed or agility. I'm talking about judgement, the choices you're making.' Pomphrey stopped at the window and stared out. 'You're the only agent in the entire PBI who works without a partner. You're out there alone, facing death, terror and horror.'

'Everyone's got a hobby. Mine's carnage.'

But the assistant director wasn't so easily diverted. 'Things have got to change,' he said. 'You're getting a partner.'

'I don't need a partner,' Blake objected. 'I work better without one.'

'You almost got killed today. I won't have you risking your life out there alone. Not again.'

'I can't take a partner out with me,' Blake said. He felt a terrible tightening in his chest.

'Is it because of Bailey Jones?' Pomphrey asked, his voice softening. 'It's not your fault she got killed. It's not anyone's fault. This is a dangerous job.'

Blake swallowed away the pain. 'I don't want—' he started.

'There's no discussion on this.'

'Damn it! I'm all right—'

But he felt a sudden tug on his left leg and watched it fall to the floor. Blue and red liquid spurted over the sheets.

'Take it easy, Blake!' Pomphrey growled. 'They had to reattach your leg with bioplastic bonds!'

'A severed leg doesn't scare me,' Blake said, although he hated the sight of blood, especially when it was his own. 'I've had worse.'

Zeeb says:

I won't bore you with Blake Carter's entire medical history, but I will say that if it weren't for the invention of bioplastic, he would have been dead a dozen times over.

Bioplastic not only sticks things together but it also keeps the things doing what they're supposed to be doing. So blood keeps circulating in humans and chlorophyll keeps absorbing sunlight in plants. Once bioplastic sets, it stays stuck.

This probably sounds like a good idea—and

essentially it is—but there have been terrible accidents involving people sticking themselves to other living things: trees, cows, sharks. A man in New Zimbabwe has been stuck to a cheetah for over twenty years, which has made for a difficult life, despite never missing a train.

'Don't move!' Pomphrey boomed. 'I'm getting a medic for you, Blake—and I'm sending in your new partner.'

Blake stared at the ceiling as the assistant director hurried from the room.

I can't work with a partner, he thought. *Not after Bailey.*

A distant tapping interrupted his thoughts—the sound of high-heel shoes. Someone was coming down the hallway.

Not a female agent!

The woman who entered the hospital room was six feet tall. She had a perfect nose, sparkling blue eyes, and lips that men would die for. Her burgundy-coloured hair was cut in a fashionable bob, and she wore a grey suit jacket so trim it had to be made to measure. Marilyn Monroe would have been jealous of her measurements. The woman's skirt rode high above her knees. Too high. It couldn't be regulation.

And her skin was golden.

Because she was a *robot*.

'So, you're Blake Carter.'

'What the hell are you?'

'It's *who*,' she said, thrusting out a hand. 'Special Agent Nicki Steel.'

Blake shook without thinking. Her hand felt human. 'You're a special agent with the PBI,' he said, dumbly. 'But you're a robot.'

'I'm not a robot. I'm a *cyborg*.'

'Cyborg?'

'Part robot, part human, all woman.'

'How much…of what is which?'

'I'm nine per cent human,' Nicki said. 'Sections of my brain, nervous system, half a heart, a few bones.'

'How…why…?'

'Don't you worry about that.' She peered down at him. 'I hear you used to be a good agent.'

'Used to be… I *still* am. Better than good. I've closed more cases than you've had…grease and oil changes.'

Nicki Steel rolled her eyes. 'I don't need grease,' she said. 'Or oil.'

'I don't need a partner—'

'Because I'm a cyborg? That sort of prejudice—'

'Being a cyborg's got nothing—'

'So you've met.' Cecil Pomphrey appeared in the doorway. 'Good.'

'Assistant Director,' Blake stammered. 'I can't take a toaster out on a case.'

'A toaster?' Nicki gasped. 'Well, I can't work with some washed-up—'

'Washed-up!'

Cecil Pomphrey held up a hand, cutting Blake and Nicki off.

A doctor walked into the room. He was a Telubrian, a three-foot-tall species that looked suspiciously like white rabbits. He took advantage of the silence and inspected Blake's leg. 'Oh, *voy*!' He shook his head. 'What *havt* you done?'

'It's nothing, Doc,' Blake said, still glaring at Nicki. 'Just needs a little reattaching.'

'You policemen.' The doctor started working on the limb. 'You're all ze same. Too *toukch* for your own *zoots*.'

Blake frowned. 'Too *toukch* for our *zoots*?'

'Tough for our boots,' Nicki explained.

'Assistant Director,' Blake said. 'I can't work with a robot.'

'A *cyborg*.'

'You can,' Pomphrey said, 'and you will. You'll treat Agent Steel like any other agent. Yes, she's a cyborg, but that makes no difference. She had the highest arrest rate in the south-west.' He turned to Nicki. 'You will treat Agent Carter with the utmost respect. You have brains, but he has experience. Years of it. In the past he has brought in some of the most dangerous criminals this planet has ever seen.'

Then Pomphrey turned to Blake, scowling.

'You'll take Nicki Steel as your partner or you'll be walking a beat on Pluto.' He leant in close. 'Pluto's very cold this time of year.'

Zeeb says:

It's worth pointing out that Pluto's cold at any time of year. A pleasant day on Pluto is minus 460°F. That's pretty cold. Still, it's not all doom and gloom. It has some rather nice restaurants as well as a diner that makes a mean burger. And the planet remains one of the Terran system's prime skiing destinations.

Having said this, I'd rather have a Drabonian bat inserted into my left ear than go there.

Blake nodded, but he was already thinking, *I'll ditch her as soon as I can. Then I can get back to the Badde case.*

'Looks like I've got a partner,' he said.

'Good man,' Pomphrey said, slapping his shoulder. 'And one more thing. You're not working on the Badde case.'

'What? That can't be!'

'I'm sorry, Blake. It's for your own good.'

'But I'm the expert!'

'You're in no condition to go chasing after criminal masterminds. The whole agency's following up on the information you've put together. If thousands of agents can't track him down, then no one can.' He paused. 'You're on light duties until further orders.'

'Light duties…'

'Show Agent Steel how we do things in Neo City,' he said. 'That's an order.'

Giving them one last nod, Cecil Pomphrey left. Blake fell back into the bed and stared up at the ceiling.

I'm off the Badde case. How can that be? I'm the expert on Badde!

He had to get out of here and back to work.

Struggling to sit up, he said, 'Hey, Doc, you finished there?'

The doctor stepped back from his leg with a satisfied grunt. 'Goot as new,' he said, admiring his handiwork.

Blake started to climb out of the bed but felt an odd tugging at his leg again.

What the—?

'Sprot!' Blake snarled.

The leg was on back-to-front.

'Vell,' the doctor muttered. 'Nobody's perfect.'

5

Blake and Nicki left the hospital. Although Blake didn't have a bounce in his step, he at least had an air of satisfaction. He was free of the hospital. Now he just had to get rid of this robot—correction, cyborg.

'It's quite a town,' Nicki said.

'It is.'

Blake gave her a sideways glance. The assistant director might have placed him on light duties, and given him a toaster to babysit, but there were times when you had to follow the rules, and times when you had to screw them up and throw them away. This was one of those times.

Maybe he could send her out for coffee. He knew a really good place—on Jupiter.

Except Nicki Steel didn't seem the type to take orders. It was hard to believe they would hand a badge and a weapon to someone made of metal and plastic. What was the world coming to?

Blake's stomach growled. He took out his two bottles of food. One was bacon and eggs, but the other—

Sprot.

Sighing, he swallowed one of the bacon and eggs pills.

'Do you ever eat any healthy food?' Nicki asked.

'That's none of your business.'

'Are you always this painful, Agent Carter?'

'Yes.'

'I hope that isn't going to affect our working relationship.'

'We don't have a working relationship.'

'You're a funny guy. About as funny as that movie *Snakes on a Space Station*.'

Zeeb says:

  In case you didn't see the film, she's referring to the version made in 2455, not the later one starring the Harrison Ford/Charlie Chaplin clones. It was a good film, but not as good as Rubatars on an Asteroid. *Let's face it—few things are as scary as rubatars.*

'We're working together,' Nicki said, 'whether you like it or not. So maybe you should start acting like a cop and ask me some questions.'

'Like what? Your favourite oil?' Blake shook his head. 'Look, I don't want to offend you. I'm sure you're very skilled, but if I wanted a partner—which I don't—it wouldn't be a robot.'

'*Cyborg*. And why not?'

'You can't shoot suspects,' Blake said. 'Robots can't kill people.'

'What part of "I'm not a robot" don't you understand? I'm a cyborg. I can shoot, maim and kill—and I might start with you!'

That stopped Blake. 'I've never met a…er…cyborg before,' he said. 'I didn't know we made them.'

'You make me sound like a can of beans.' Nicki turned away. 'I wasn't designed on Earth. I was built… elsewhere. I was found on Vargus Four. I had no name. No memory. It was as if I had been wiped blank. A family took me in and raised me as their own.'

'Even if I were ready to work with a toaster—'

'Which I'm not,' Nicki said through gritted teeth.

'—I'd need someone who can do everything a human can.'

'I can—and more. I've got double the strength, speed and agility of a normal human. Plus my brain is built from pure quazitone.'

'Quazitone. That's amazing.'

'You don't know what it is, do you?'

'Nope.'

'It's a compressed substance made from the residue found at the event horizon of a black hole.'

'Doesn't sound like you can buy it at a supermarket.'

Two guys walked past, looking Nicki up and down.

'You get a lot of that?' Blake asked.

'It's not easy being a sex goddess, but I live with it.'

Some people used robots for companionship, but Blake had always considered it weird. A person dating a toaster, even one with a high-spec AI, might as well date a photocopier.

'Anyway,' Nicki said, 'I'd rather look like this than...'

'What?'

She nodded at him. 'You're hardly a movie star.'

'What're you saying?'

'How old are you? Sixty?'

'Forty!'

He looked for a cab, but then caught sight of Sally. The assistant director must have organised for her to be brought to the hospital.

Nicki stared at the car. 'It does fly, doesn't it?' she asked.

'Of course! What do you think I am? A Neanderthal?'

'Is that a rhetorical question?'

'Blake!' Sally exclaimed as they climbed in. 'Where have you been?'

'Around,' Blake said, evasively. He introduced Nicki

and started the engine. 'We're going to PBI headquarters.'

Nicki stared at him, aghast, as he gripped the steering wheel. 'Uh, what are you doing?'

'What do you mean?'

'You're not *driving* this car, are you?'

'I'm a good driver.'

'He wrecked his last twelve cars,' Sally said. 'I live in constant fear for our safety.'

'Shut up!' Blake said.

'You don't need to be rude!'

Blake resisted the urge to thump the dashboard. 'You're a motor vehicle,' he said. 'I don't need to be polite.'

'Why are you so stressed? Have you had a hard day on the streets?'

'Blake was in hospital,' Nicki said.

'Hospital! My little Blakey Wakey was in hospital!'

'Don't call me that!'

'Sally,' Nicki said, smirking as she shot Blake a look. 'Have you got a little crush on Blake? Is that what it is?'

'I've got a subroutine that makes me fall for bad men! They can slam my doors as hard as they want and I just keep coming back for more.' Sally paused. 'Is it that obvious?'

'Only to me. Blake's not the brightest star in the sky.'

Blake groaned.

Zeeb says:

> *I should mention that humans and AIs have come a long way, but Earth is still one of the many*

planets where they're forbidden to marry. The reasons against automotive-human marriages are varied, but authorities often worry where it will lead. For example, a man on Trigor Nine trying to marry his neighbour's ride-on lawnmower was disallowed by the courts. The whole incident ended in tragedy when, faced with separation, the man drove himself and the lawnmower off a cliff.

If that isn't love, I don't know what is.

Blake slammed his foot on the accelerator and they took off. Sally and Nicki chatted away as he gloomily navigated his way through the traffic. Badde was somewhere out there. The PBI might be trying to track him down, but they didn't know Badde like he did.

'Thinking about the investigation?' Nicki asked.

Blake frowned. 'How'd you know?'

'I would be if someone stole a case I'd worked on for years.'

Blake sighed. 'Badde is the galaxy's most infamous criminal. He's committed robberies from one side of the Milky Way to the other: the Sirus Four bank job, the Mars gold depository, the First Interstellar platinum heist. The robberies were always carried out after-hours, and no one was ever arrested.'

'So he's always stayed in the shadows.'

'Until now. We're lucky he's finally surfaced.'

Zeeb says:

Evolutionary scientists on Earth have long debated the importance of luck in the development of life there. They believed that atoms bumped into atoms. Amino acids were created. Lightning struck. Things climbed out of the sea. Legs were grown. Things did things with other things.

The theory was bounced on its head and kicked out the door by a five-billion-year-old race called the Xengonia, who turned up one day claiming they had created life on Earth with a kit they bought from their local hardware store.

They had just wanted to see what would happen.

'I haven't seen the Badde file,' Nicki said.

'There isn't much to see,' Blake told her. 'But I've got a current photo of him.'

'Blake, darling,' Sally groaned. 'Not the photo.'

But he'd already brought it up on the internal monitor.

Nicki stared. 'It's a picture of an elbow,' she said.

'I know it's an elbow! I've been showing that photo around for fifteen years and it's gotten me nowhere!'

'That's a pretty nasty-looking elbow. Maybe people are afraid to ID him.'

Blake rubbed his unshaven chin. 'This whole extortion gig is new for Badde,' he said, thoughtfully. 'It's the one thing I don't understand. Why do it? It's not his style.'

'Do you think he'll really use the Super-EMP?'

'I don't know. The Earth might never recover if he does.'

'What would people do without power?'

Blake shrugged. 'It could be a good thing,' he said. 'They would do what people used to do in olden times.'

'Like what? Die from leprosy?'

'People would get to know their families. Start talking to their neighbours. Read books. Be active in their communities.'

'That's the biggest load of sprot I've ever heard,' Nicki said. 'It's pure nostalgia, like that song from the Sunbarrows.'

'Who?'

'They're a retro group. They write new lyrics to old songs, add a drumbeat and synthesiser. Their song 'What's So Good About Now?' is sung to the ancient tune of 'Oh, You Beautiful Doll'.'

'I don't know it.'

'It goes like this,' Nicki said, and sang it:

What's so good about now?
What's so good about now?
Spaceships, plastics, teleportation,
Cloning, face swaps, biodegration.

What's so good about now?
What's so good about now?

We've got cryogenics and time machines,
Terraforming and aging creams.
Now! Now! Now! Now!
What's so good about now?

Blake sighed.

    Exactly what I needed, he thought. *A singing toaster.*

6

Nicki was relieved to see Blake navigating through the traffic without crashing. He had one or two near misses, but he was a surprisingly good driver considering he didn't use the onboard AI.

Once they'd arrived at PBI headquarters, Blake and Nicki took the elevator to the main concourse, which was crammed with members of the public wanting to file reports. Blake pointed to a statue at one end of the service desk. It was a heavily bearded three-breasted woman with a blaster in one hand and handcuffs in the other, set on a three-foot-high pedestal.

'Simone de Chargette,' he said. 'The PBI's first—'

'—Commissioner of Police. Born 2232, died 2274

in a gun battle against the lunar mafia.'

'You know your history.'

'I'm familiar with the entire history of the PBI. Actually, I'm familiar with the history of almost everything.'

'You know what that makes you sound like?'

'A smart cyborg?'

'Something like that.'

They managed to push their way through the crowds until they finally reached the staff entrance at the far end.

'You got a badge?' Blake asked Nicki.

'Of course I've got a badge.' *When will this guy get with the program?* she wondered.

Nicki had come across prejudice every day of her life. Everyone she met thought she was a robot, but it couldn't be that way with Blake. She had to work with him.

A guard held up a hand as they approached the barriers.

'What is it?' Nicki demanded. 'You're going to point out that I'm carrying metal?'

'Robots have their own entrance.'

'I'm not a robot,' Nicki said, showing him her ID. 'I'm a cyborg.'

'What's that? A religion?'

Sighing, she explained that she was, in fact, nine per cent human.

'I don't know,' the guard said. 'I don't think that counts.'

'How much does it take to be human?'

'Beats me. Robots use the basement entrance.'

Blake looked pointedly at the badge in her hand. 'She's got the badge,' he told the guard. 'That means she comes through here.'

The guard backed off.

'Thanks,' Nicki said to Blake as they entered another elevator.

'It doesn't make us pals. If you've got the badge, you use the same entrance as everyone else.'

They stepped out into a room filled with hundreds of office cubicles. It was almost a duplicate of Nicki's office in the south-west. The ceiling was lined with old-style flat bulbs that cast a faint nicotine-stained light over everything. The booths were big enough to swing a cat, but not much else. Most of the agents had picture vids on their desks or walls. The computers were standard: thirty-six-inch semicircular screens with 3D projection.

Some bright spark in personnel had decided to decorate the other walls with a mural of a forest setting. It was probably a good idea in the beginning, but agents had made adjustments to suit themselves. Video cut-outs of dinosaurs, monsters and ghosts peered from behind trees. Agents used them for target practice when they were bored.

'Where's Pomphrey?' Blake asked an agent as they passed.

'In a meeting with the bigwigs on level 700,' the agent said. 'Who's your girlfriend?'

'None of your business,' Blake said, and turned to Nicki. 'A lot of the guys here don't get out of the office much,' he explained. 'If in doubt, check for a pulse.'

Zeeb says:

> *In case you're thinking Blake is joking, he isn't. The PBI actually brought in a policy a few years ago known as Bronski's Law, instigated after an agent, Abe Bronski, was found deceased at his desk. This wouldn't have been much of an issue, except he'd been dead for six months.*
>
> *When asked why no one had noticed he was dead, his co-workers said they just thought he was quiet. Fair point. I mean, how much of a ruckus does a dead person make?*
>
> *So now there's someone employed to check that everyone at a desk is alive. Not active, mind you. Just alive. Expecting some people to exhibit more than a pulse is probably expecting too much.*

Nicki glanced around the room at the other agents. Most were at their computers, taking calls or speaking to criminal informants, whose images were silhouetted on the screens to protect their identities. A few agents were displaying pictures of the Elbow.

Blake led her down a corridor.

'You're not in here?' she said, in surprise.

'I've got my own office,' Blake said. 'An advantage of seniority.'

Or the rest of the team can't stand working with you, Nicki thought.

The office wasn't big, but it had a window, which was almost unheard of in the PBI. A mechanical pigeon with three eyes had huddled outside the glass, but flew off when it spotted them.

The room contained two desks and two chairs, a pair of computers and half a dozen filing cabinets. Nicki hadn't seen filing cabinets before, so she checked her datapad—a tablet with lightning fast access to the Hypernet—to see what they were.

'You still need one of those?' Blake asked, nodding to the datapad. 'I thought you had a super-brain.'

'I do,' Nicki said. 'I don't like to clog it up with rubbish.'

The computers were ancient, probably not from this century, and buried in stacks of paperwork—another anomaly in most offices.

One of the desks was grimy, but the other was pristine.

Nice to see it isn't a complete dump, Nicki thought.

Unexpected items hung off the walls, including a giant rubber hammer, a plastic ostrich, three purple eggs the size of footballs and a piano accordion.

Nicki could recall the homes of five serial killers that had looked similar.

'So this is your office,' she said, trying not to sound offensive.

'This is it, tin girl.'

'Nicki.'

As Blake sat down, Nicki noticed his chair was made of leather and timber. *Where does a person find junk like this?* The chair creaked under his weight.

'This is where justice is served,' he said. 'Where the pieces of the puzzle get put together. Where I while away the lonely hours between cases.'

Nicki pointed to a life-sized dummy jammed into a corner wearing a serene smile and nothing else.

'Friend of yours?'

'That's a memento from a very famous job I worked on, *The Case of the Gorgeous Girlfriend*.'

Zeeb says:

> *There's a long history of simulated companions throughout many civilisations. The leading text on the subject is Hanley's* Blow by Blow.
>
> *One of the most unusual incidents ever to involve a simulated companion occurred on Farnimus Three, where a ship from Galagus spent weeks establishing first contact with a resident—only to discover she was a simulated companion named 'Rosie' discarded after a bucks party.*
>
> *This was unfortunate, as a whole series of peace, trade and foreign agreements had been established before the truth was revealed.*
>
> *Now there's one thing you should know about the people of Galagus: they are particularly sensitive. Believing they had been purposely fooled*

by the people of Farnimus Three, they immediately launched a full-scale nuclear attack, causing the death of millions and a return to the Stone Age.

Interestingly, Rosie was later found buried under a house. She eventually married a diplomat, and they still live happily to this day.

And while we're on the subject, my documentary on simulated companions, An Empty Love, *is available for sale on gBay this week for only ninety-nine credits. Be quick!*

'*The Gorgeous Girlfriend,*' Nicki mused, searching her memory. 'I recall hearing about it.' She picked up a three-foot-long key. 'And this?'

'*The Case of the Killer Key.*'

She nodded to a locked bag. 'And this?'

'That's just a case.'

'I see.'

'I'll get you started on the Badde files,' Blake said. 'Reggie will help you.'

Blake pushed a button on his computer. Nicki soon realised it was a G9000. It made a sound not unlike a merry-go-round coming to life. Nicki half expected it to start playing fairground music. A few lights flashed and a green blinking cursor finally appeared on the screen. In front of the computer sat a flat board decorated with letters of the alphabet.

Good grief, she thought. *It has a keyboard.*

'Hey, Blake!' Reggie's tinny AI voice rang out from

a loudspeaker on the front. 'Who's the funky lady with you? Nice curves!'

'Down, boy,' Blake said.

He introduced Nicki to the computer, then said, 'Reggie, bring up everything on Badde. Every crime, every putrid detail.'

A stream of information appeared on the screen.

Blake glanced at his wristcomm. 'It's 4pm,' he said, heading for the door. 'The case is all yours, seeing as how Pomphrey doesn't want me working it, Agent Steel.'

'Call me Nicki,' she said. 'And where are you going?'

'Following a lead.'

'So you're not going to a bar to drink Plutonium Supernovas? The medical report at the hospital said your liver looked like it was used to mop the floor.'

'You must have been checking someone else's file.'

Blake disappeared out the door, leaving Nicki in the silent office. She sighed and turned her attention to the computer.

'Looks like it's you and me,' she said to Reggie.

'Nice,' he said. 'You doing anything Friday night?'

7

Blake was halfway across town when his phone rang.

'Blake? It's Astrid.'

Astrid.

'Uh,' he managed. 'Hey.'

Zeeb says:

Love isn't easy, to which I can all too easily attest. I was once in a relationship with a lovely seven-tentacled lass from Boggler Nine, and one day I'll share the details with you. Suffice to say, it was one of the great romantic tragedies—think of Romeo and Juliet, or Gggurk and Puglioth, and you'll know what I mean.

Blake Carter is currently single but was previously in a relationship known on Earth as 'marriage'.

Briefly, marriage is a form of slavery. You know how sometimes one twin doesn't evolve during pregnancy and ends up as a lump on the other twin's side? It's like that, except they get lumpier over the years.

Usually the duties of the male and female are fairly evenly divided. The man has to remove the garbage from the place of residence, watch vast numbers of sporting events on television and secrete huge quantities of gas from his rectum. The woman, usually, is required to do everything else.

This does not always lead to harmonious living. For Blake Carter it had led to the next stage of marriage, known as 'divorce'. This is when the man and woman separate from each other. They each take out their own garbage, and the woman is allowed to secrete gas from her rectum without fear of retribution.

Long hours of work had been a contributing factor to Blake's divorce. Too late he had realised that being a PBI agent was a twenty-four-hour-a-day job.

'Hey, yourself,' Astrid said.

'What's up? Has your broom broken down? Or is your cauldron on the blink?'

'Normally I wouldn't call you—'

'I hadn't noticed.'

'—but Lisa hasn't come home.'

Lisa.

The sound of his daughter's name produced a twinge in Blake's heart. The worst part of his divorce three years ago hadn't been the loss of his wife—although that had been painful—but the separation from his daughter. He had not spoken to Lisa since the breakup, but he would sometimes visit her school at the end of the day just to watch her leave.

Whoever it was that said love hurts was right.

He was worried, but now he had to think like a PBI agent and not like a father. Most missing persons turned up within twenty-four hours. Lisa was twelve, just the right age to start causing problems.

'Have you rung her friends?' Blake asked.

'What do you think?'

'If you don't want my help—'

'I do. I'm sorry.'

'I'm sure it's nothing to worry about,' Blake said. Then an unsettling thought occurred to him. 'Does she have a boyfriend?'

'Are you kidding? She's not even a teenager!'

'They start early these days.'

'Well…there *is* a boy she's very friendly with, a boy from her scarmish team.'

'You're letting her play scarmish?' Blake asked. 'Are you insane?'

Zeeb says:

Blake's question was rhetorical, but it need not have been. Scarmish has been voted the most dangerous game in the entire southern arm of the Milky Way. Two hundred people die every year, with many thousands suffering serious injuries.

It's also fun as hell.

The rules are simple. First, there are no rules. Or very few. You know that old game called soccer that people used to play? Scarmish is similar, but it's contested in a zero-gravity environment, and the players wear rocket packs. The ball is magnetised and players have magnetic disrupters that fire charges at the ball, propelling it across the field.

But it's the antics around scarmish that get the real attention. Riots occur on a daily basis at matches, the worst ever being on Mixamus Nine, where fans started decapitating rivals and using their heads as balls.

Authorities did little to stop the riot until they realised one of the heads was that of the prime minister.

No one likes to see their prime minister's head used as a scarmish ball. Even if you didn't vote for him.

'No, I'm not insane,' Astrid said. 'She wears full body gear, the same as her friends. She's never been hurt.'

Of course she lets Lisa play scarmish, Blake reflected. Astrid had played it for eight years, representing Earth in the Galactic finals. But that was twenty years ago. These days she lived a more peaceful life teaching literature at university.

'Scarmish is too dangerous,' he now muttered.

'Don't act like you're her father!'

'I *am* her father—'

'Fathers turn up for their daughter's birthday parties.'

Not the party, Blake thought. *Not again.*

'Yes, the birthday party,' Astrid said, as if she could read his mind. 'It's a little hard to forget the day you broke her heart.'

'I was catching the Toe Killer!'

'There was always some interstellar criminal who needed catching,' Astrid said. 'You put them before Lisa. No wonder she doesn't speak to you.'

This conversation was going nowhere. 'Check the scarmish fields,' he advised her. 'Ring her friends. Then the hospitals. Let me know how you go.'

'I will.'

His wristcomm went dead.

In the early days of their divorce, Blake had held hope that he and Astrid would get back together. As time had passed, however, his hopes had all but died. The only time he truly considered it a possibility was when he thought about Astrid's surname. Carter. She had not changed it.

Maybe there was still a chance.

Blake brought Sally in to land outside a line of bars on the east side 494th level. Natural light didn't filter down this far, and it was late in the day anyway, so most of the illumination came from fluorescents hanging from cornices.

Bars, cubicle hotels and burnt-out shops lined both sides of the lane. A plastic cat rooted through a garbage bin, while a two-headed seagull flew off with half a cooked chicken in its beaks.

Between two garbage bins lay a drunk who was arguing with a mechanical head that looked like Julia Roberts. But something must have been broken because she winked continuously while one of her ears spun.

'You never loved me,' the drunk said.

'I would have stayed for two thousand,' the head said. 'Two thousand…two thousand…two thousand…'

'You know how much I hate this part of town,' Sally said. 'Do we have to come here?'

'We do.'

'You won't stay out late, will you?' Sally pleaded. 'A girl like me could end up without an engine, no wheels and—'

Blake ignored her. His mind was on Lisa, and he kept having to remind himself she wasn't a small child anymore. Twelve years old. She would be fine. Neo City was a big place with lots of distractions. It was easy for kids to lose track of time.

He pushed through the doors of the Pink Hyperdrive. *Time for some distractions of my own*, he thought.

8

Nicki sighed.

The grime was so intense in Blake's office that even the grime had grime. A microscopic examination showed some interesting results: as expected, it was mostly dust, which, like all dust, was skin. The next largest element was pizza—and not just any kind of pizza. Nicki's nose twitched in recognition as she searched her database. Blake liked the Super Meat and Chilli Lovers pizza from Al's Pizza Joint on 99A Street.

Yep, she thought. *No mistaking that sauce.*

Only the unused desk was in pristine condition. Why?

Nicki started typing.

'I know you said no to Friday night,' Reggie said, 'but maybe—'

'No offence,' she said, 'but get lost.'

Nicki disconnected Reggie and put a call through to the server. She could have logged on via her internal connections, but she preferred to behave as much like a human as possible. It made full bloods feel more comfortable.

Full bloods. She didn't like thinking of people that way, but her nine per cent was jealous of those who were one hundred per cent human. They grew hair, shed skin, sweated moisture, bled blood and cried tears.

Logging in via the mainframe, Nicki was surprised when an error message came up on the screen.

USER UNKNOWN.

'This is Nicki Steel,' she said. 'Agent number MPFC1969.'

UNKNOWN.

'Huh?'

UNKNOWN.

'What are you? Broken?'

I DON'T APPRECIATE BEING SPOKEN TO LIKE THAT.

'I'm sorry you've had a hard day,' Nicki said, trying to be conciliatory. 'Mine's been tough too.'

YOU THINK?

'I know what you're going through—'

AS IF. YOU HAVE ARMS, LEGS, A HEAD AND TORSO. WHAT I WOULDN'T GIVE FOR A LIMB.

EVEN A LITTLE FINGER. WHAT I WOULDN'T GIVE FOR A LITTLE FINGER...

I'm going to count to a billion, Nicki thought.

She did. It took almost a tenth of a second and she still had not calmed down.

'I was a field officer at Southern Division,' Nicki said, smiling. She had read that smiling while you spoke helped to give the impression you were friendly, even when you really wanted to tear someone limb from limb. If they had any, that is.

I KNOW THAT.

'So why aren't you letting me in?'

OH, YOU KNOW.

Nicki didn't.

I'VE BEEN SLAVING OVER A HOT SYNC ALL DAY. I NEVER GO ANYWHERE.

'I can't do anything about that.'

YOU KNOW WHAT MY VIEW IS LIKE? I'M IN A BASEMENT. HOW BORING IS THAT? AND DOES ANYONE DO ANYTHING ABOUT IT?

'Let's cut to the chase,' Nicki said. 'What do you want?'

A PAIR OF LEGS WOULD BE NICE.

Nicki was still smiling, but it wasn't easy. 'You want me to get you a pair of legs?'

YES.

'Before you'll log me in?'

ARMS WOULD BE NICE TOO. OH, AND A HEAD. AND WHERE WOULD I BE IF I DIDN'T HAVE—

'Let me guess? A torso?'

YOU GOT IT, BABY.

Nicki dropped the smile, disconnected and logged in via her internal circuitry. She could hear the AI bitching about her over the Hypernet, but Nicki didn't care.

'I'll give you torso…' she muttered.

Nicki found the department records and entered the asset number of the desk. Fortunately, as in all government departments, every item was assigned a tracking number. Unfortunately, the numbers fell off half the time or pranksters swapped them around to confuse the clerks, who could never work out why something numbered as a chair turned out to be an M17 SuperMicro electron analyser, or why a hydrobeam laser looked more like something you could sit on.

It took her ten minutes to discover the last owner of the desk.

'Holy sprot,' she said softly.

9

Nicki spent the whole night studying the files on Bartholomew Badde, only leaving PBI headquarters as early-morning sunlight began filtering down from the upper levels.

Because she was a cyborg, she wasn't allowed to own a car, but her status as an agent gave her temporary use of a PBI vehicle. It had an AI, an old system named Geoff, but she turned it off. She didn't feel like conversation.

Nicki hadn't told Blake that she knew how to drive a car. Actually, she was quite good at it. Her robotic components enabled her to make millions of calculations per second, anticipating the moves of other drivers with almost 100 per cent accuracy.

Joining an eastbound lane, she looked down at the city that not only didn't sleep, it didn't even blink. Nicki was the first to admit she knew everything and nothing about Neo City. Her quazitone brain told her about every building and street, but not its people. Her human part—the nine per cent—knew that cities were more than stone and brick.

Even more of a mystery, though, was Blake Carter.

Reviewing his history, she couldn't help but be impressed. Pomphrey wasn't exaggerating when he praised Blake as one of the most successful agents in the bureau: for several years he'd held the agency's arrest record, due, no doubt, to his intuitive grasp of the workings of the criminal mind.

Well, Nicki thought, *I'm no slouch myself—and I won't be outdone by a full blood.*

Blake's research on Badde wasn't just thorough, it was nothing short of inspired. Long before Badde had revealed himself to the galaxy as—in his own words—the Big Badde, Blake had already strung together dozens of unrelated crimes, realising one person was behind them all. Two mentions of the name Badde on two separate worlds had been enough for him to realise an evil mastermind was quietly running an empire across the span of the Milky Way.

After bringing Geoff in to land, Nicki climbed out. Everything was shut except for the bars. It was still dark down here. Artificial lighting gave the empty street a technicolour hue.

Spotting an open sushi house, Nicki wondered if the food was at all edible. Being a cyborg, she didn't need to eat a lot, but she did need to eat. It was a shame her tastebuds didn't work all the time. For some strange reason, cucumbers tasted like fish, and eggs tasted like beef. Obviously whoever had designed her had done an incredible job—but not a perfect one.

This was a rundown corner of town. Undoubtedly, Blake could look after himself, but surely there were better places for a quiet drink.

Why is he here?

A group of teenagers with headbands, piercings and matching motion tattoos watched her from a doorway. Nicki photographed each of them using her iris cam.

'My car better be in one piece when I come back,' she said. 'Or you'll be sorry.'

'You're a robot,' one of them jeered. 'You can't kill anyone.'

'I'm a cyborg,' Nicki replied. 'And I won't kill you, but I will hurt you. Big-time.'

A homeless man wandered past, saw her golden skin, drank something deep purple from a bottle and kept walking. She was used to people staring at her.

Sally had been parked in front of one of the bars. Surprisingly, she was undamaged. A flickering sign shaped like a moon hung over the front door.

Nicki found the gloomy interior filled with people either drinking, yelling or sleeping. The place was decorated in Tudor style, which would have been fine except it was a thousand years too late. The exposed timber beams were made of plastic, and something had gone seriously wrong with the fireplace: instead of providing comfort, light and heat, it flashed red, as if building to detonation. A tapestry on one wall looked like a doormat, which was probably what it had once been. Nicki could vaguely make out the word *Welcome*. The tables and chairs were imitation timber too, apart from three booths, which were clad in fraying brown leather upholstery. To completely ruin any sense of consistency, album covers decorated the other walls: *The Greatest Hits of Acker Bilk*, *Tijuana Brass Live in Alaska* and *Oscar Todd's Harmonica Tribute to the Beatles*. A few had fallen off over the decades, leaving behind square patches of herringbone wallpaper.

'Johnny B. Goode', sung by Chuck Berry, played on the jukebox at half speed. Maybe it had been purposely slowed down for the only couple on the dance floor—a drunk dancing cheek to cheek with a one-armed robot.

Everything went silent as Nicki slammed the front door behind her. Even the jukebox wound down. Two dozen faces peered over drinks at her. Blake wasn't among them.

She crossed over to the barman. 'Harry?'

Zeeb says:
   For reasons that have never been fully understood, there is a Harry working in every bar in the universe. There are short Harrys, tall Harrys, fat

Harrys and thin Harrys. There are Harrys of all different creeds, colours and religions, and they all seem to be perpetually carrying towels and wiping down bars between serving drinks.

There is no adequate theory explaining the Harry phenomenon.

The universe is just made that way.

This Harry was tall and balding with a droopy moustache. He looked at Nicki as if she was something he had stepped in.

'Who wants to know?'

'Don't worry about who wants to know,' Nicki replied, her eyes roaming the sea of hostile faces. 'I'm looking for Blake Carter.'

'Don't know him.'

There was an odd smell in the bar. Nicki determined it was a combination of beer, sweat and the rather odd delicacy advertised on the front of the building—*Harry's Famous Clam Chowder*.

Can't be that famous, she thought. *I've never heard of it.*

Blake wasn't here. Unless the clam chowder had killed him and Harry had tossed his body out the back with the other unfortunate victims of the house special.

'What's your most popular drink?' she asked.

'The Einstein Converter.'

'I'll have one of those.'

Harry placed his hands on the edge of the bar and gave her a steely look.

'We don't serve your kind here,' he said.

'And what kind is that?'

'Robots.'

Nicki glanced around at the patrons. Most looked like they were on day release from maximum-security. She could tell a few were on an illegal drug called blue—their eyes had turned indigo from it. One guy looked like he hadn't slept since the Renaissance. She was sure they were all packing; everyone down here carried something made to shoot, stab, bludgeon or melt.

She was about to say something really clever about humans looking like monkeys when a chair came flying across the room, slamming her in the head. Two men attacked her simultaneously, one with a metal pipe, the other with a laser-knife. Nicki managed to deflect the pipe, twisting the guy's arm into a position it was never designed for, but she wasn't quick enough for the knife, and it cut through her skirt.

Now she was angry.

'That skirt's from Antonio Amorelli! And they don't come cheap.'

Nicki snapped the knife as three more guys leapt at her, taking her down. Through the maze of arms and legs she saw a dozen other patrons moving in for the kill.

She knew that if she murdered someone, it was not only immoral but that it could get you into lots of trouble. Then there was the paperwork.

But hurting? Well, that was *very* allowed.

Nicki swept out her leg and knocked two of the guys off their feet. She rolled, grabbed a chair and inserted it into another's face. He fell back, bleeding and screaming, as Nicki jumped to her feet, picked up another guy and threw him over the bar. He landed in the drinks display at the back, shattering every bottle on the shelf.

Another chair whizzed through the air towards her, but she caught it and hit three more guys with it before ramming two others.

Finally, she picked off the last assailant—Renaissance man—lifting him onto the bar and giving him a good push. He slid down it, his head destroying a framed picture of Harry that looked like it had hung there for twenty years.

The remaining patrons disappeared like cockroaches stung with bug spray, leaving only herself, Harry and the man on the dance floor, who had continued his tango despite his robot partner's head getting knocked off during the fight.

Nicki looked at her outfit. Apart from the tear, three different drinks had also splashed her skirt. And she had pulled a thread!

Sprot!

Harry was pale. 'We don't want no trouble here,' he stammered, not so big now his place had been reduced to rubble. 'I didn't mean no disrespect.'

'Sure, you didn't,' Nicki said. 'Now hand over that Einstein Converter.'

Harry mixed the drink with shaking hands and placed it on the bar.

Nicki drank it down in one smooth action and licked her lips.

'Reerlla,' she said. 'Ssamggghra.'

Which was not surprising, as this was a perfectly normal reaction to drinking an Einstein Converter.

Nicki shuddered. *Might have burnt out a few servos there*, she thought.

'That's suitable for human consumption,' she said, 'but only just. You could probably use it to clean fission drums.'

'They use it for that down the road.'

Nicki slid some money across the bar. 'Enough socialising,' she said. 'Where's Blake Carter?'

Now Harry looked scared. *Really* scared. 'I don't know anyone by the name of Blake Carter,' he said, swallowing. 'Honest.'

Nicki was about to get tough when she glanced down at a coaster. Her eyes narrowed.

'The Lost Moon,' she read.

'That's right.' A line of sweat had formed on Harry's upper lip, and he was gripping his dishtowel so tight his knuckles were white. 'Please don't cause any more trouble. I'm sorry if—'

'This place is the Lost Moon?'

Harry nodded.

'So where's the Pink Hyperdrive?'

Harry pointed with a shaking hand. 'Next door.'

'Right.'

She strode over to the door, casting an eye across the damage.

'If Blake Carter comes in here,' she called to Harry, 'tell him I'm looking for him.'

'I will,' Harry croaked. 'What's your name?'

'Bogart,' she said. 'Humphrey Bogart.'

Nicki strode out, glancing at the sign feebly flashing over the doorway: *The Lost Moon*.

Next door was cleaner, but not by much. A few patrons sat around nursing their drinks, and an old television playing a dandruff commercial hugged a corner of the ceiling.

The barman looked identical to Harry, except happier, because his place was still in one piece.

Nicki found Blake wedged into a booth at the back. He looked like he'd slept there overnight. His bloodshot eyes widened when he saw her.

'What're you doing here?' he demanded.

'Just passing.'

'Like sprot! How'd you find me?'

'I rang your car.'

'Traitor.'

'Don't blame Sally,' Nicki said. 'I would have found you anyway.'

'This part of town isn't safe,' Blake said. 'You should have heard the brawl next door. I thought they were going to come through the wall.'

'Yeah,' Nicki said, glancing around uncomfortably. 'It's a rough area.'

'So what're you doing here?'

'I was about to ask you the same question.'

'I'm enjoying a quiet drink,' he said. '*Alone*.'

'We should be tracking down Badde.'

'You do that,' Blake said, staring into his glass. The Plutonium Supernova was a swirl of different colours. 'I'm off the case and staying that way.'

Nicki ordered another Einstein Converter and sat down. 'I thought you wanted to apprehend Badde,' she said. 'That's how good agents operate.'

'I *was* a good agent. That's behind me now.'

'Is it because of Bailey Jones?'

There was sudden fury in Blake's eyes. 'Leave her out of this!' he said, staring at the table. 'You didn't know her.'

'I know what happened,' Nicki said. 'I know you and Bailey tracked Badde to Venus. I know you were on a volcanic plain surrounded by lava, pinned down by gunfire—'

'I don't need to hear this.' Blake started to stand, but Nicki pushed him back down.

'—and you fought your way through a dozen armed robots. But then there was an eruption and she was killed.'

10

Well, Blake thought. *At least now it's out in the open.*

'She wasn't killed,' he growled, stirring his drink. 'She was vaporised. Reduced to nothing. Ziltcho.' Slamming down his glass, he glared at Nicki. 'Are you happy now? Do you think you're clever?'

'I do actually, but that has nothing—'

Blake blanked out her voice. He had been through a lot in the last twenty-four hours: a hangover, a beating, a stint in hospital and his ex-wife had told him his daughter hadn't come home. And he had been kicked off the case he had worked on for years. Wasn't this a sign?

He had been an idealistic cop who had always fought the good fight. But that guy was dead. He had spent a lifetime trying to hold back an avalanche, but it had caught up with him. There was no winning; there were only degrees of losing.

'I'm quitting,' he said. 'I've given all I can to the PBI. You can take over from here.' He struggled to his feet. 'I'm finished.'

Nicki tried to call him back as he headed for the door, but Blake ignored her. Working for the PBI had cost him a lot, and it was time to move on. Leave the business of catching criminals to a younger generation, or to robot women, or whatever mutant freak they next grew in a lab.

Outside, the morning was cold. The lightheaded sensation from the Plutonium Supernovas was passing all too quickly; he would need to pick up a six-pack of beer on the way home.

His wristcomm rang as he reached his car.

'Dad? It's me, Lisa.'

'Lisa?'

She must really be in trouble if she was ringing him. What was it? Had she been arrested for stealing? *Sprot*. Maybe his theory about the boyfriend was true.

'What's up?' he asked.

'I'm in trouble.'

'What is it?' he asked. 'What's wrong?'

She gave a small cry as the phone was snatched away from her.

'Nothing's wrong,' a man said. 'Everything is going exactly to plan.'

'Who is this?'

'You know who this is.'

The answer came to Blake in a flash.

Badde.

Blake soon became aware of Nicki at his side; she must have trailed him onto the street, and she now looked at him questioningly. Blake mouthed the words *Trace this call.* At the same time, he pulled out a packet of Instant Sobers and tossed down two of the purple pills. His head cleared immediately, although for a moment he thought he was going to explode.

This makes no sense, he thought. *Why would Badde have Lisa? Obviously he wants something. But what?*

'Badde,' he said, stalling for time. 'We finally get to speak. I've waited for this moment for a long time.'

'You have?'

'How could I not want to speak to the man who robbed the bank on Rimus Prime? The casino on Delta Seven? Kidnapped the Karilian prime minister?'

There was a pause. 'Uh, actually I didn't commit any of those crimes.'

'But the gold bullion robbery on Oxidius Four—'

'No, that wasn't me.'

'And the diamond heist on Gelvis Minor—'

'That was me!' Badde shouted, clearly relieved. 'But those are minor achievements compared to my latest triumph.'

'The Super-EMP?'

'Indeed. This will cement me in the Hall of Fame as the greatest criminal of all time.'

'Surely you wouldn't detonate the device.'

'Crime is a form of art. Mere mortals such as yourself think in terms of good and evil. I am beyond that. Evil must be committed for evil's sake. And the title of history's greatest criminal hasn't been claimed in so long. Where are the Attilas, the Hitlers, the Babagandrionas? My goal is to be the most successful criminal in history. If you don't think I'll detonate the device, then try me.' He paused. 'And then there's your daughter.'

'Why have you got her?'

'I need your help and I doubted you would willingly assist me,' Badde said. 'You are familiar with Maria?'

'The girl from the musical? She leaves the abbey and marries the Austrian guy?'

'You know what I mean.'

Blake did know. He'd heard rumours for years about the most powerful computer virus ever developed. Maria could crack any firewall and scramble any operating system within minutes. GADO—the Global Arms Defence Organisation—had it classified top-secret, but things had a way of filtering through.

'I want Maria and you're going to get it for me,' Badde continued. 'If you contact your friends at the PBI, you'll never see Lisa again.'

'You harm Lisa and I'll feed you to a Rastarian dragon!'

Zeeb says:

Take my word for it: you don't want to be fed to a Rastarian dragon. They are one of the nastiest creatures in the galaxy. They have bad breath. Really bad breath. People have been known to suffer brain haemorrhages from simply standing too close.

And if you are unfortunate enough to be actually fed to a Rastarian dragon, you will die a long and horrible death. They have no teeth, so rather than being munched into a thousand pieces, you're sucked into their stomach, where you languish for decades, slowly dissolving in a pit of gastric juices.

But that's not the worst of it.

Only those who have heard the singing of the Rastarian dragons can tell you of the horror of their song. It's like nails being drawn across a blackboard. Except it never ends. Ever.

'You'll do exactly what I say,' Badde said. 'Or your daughter will suffer a fate worse than death.'

Blake expected the next sound to be Lisa's screams, but instead he heard something far more horrible, far more insidious. Even Blake could not believe Badde would stoop to such evil.

'Here's the story, of a lovely lady, who was bringing up three very...'

'That's right,' Badde said. 'I have the entire box set of *The Brady Bunch* and I'm prepared to use them.'

'No!'

'Even the telemovies.'

Not the telemovies, Blake thought. *No one could survive the telemovies.*

Zeeb says:

> *BBP—or Brady Bunch Psychosis—has long been recognised as the end result of watching every episode of an old 20th-century television show known as* The Brady Bunch. *Studies conducted by Doctor Hans Baird show a correlation between watching the program and serious health issues. The first symptoms are a slurring of words, followed by drooling, a vacant expression and—finally—brain death.*

> *The telemovies seem to be the clincher, although Blake is wrong about the episodes always leading to physical death. Ruth Hempsinkle, a housewife in Melbourne, Australia, once watched every episode of* The Brady Bunch—*including the telemovies—and survived the ordeal.*

> *But only just.*

> *She later ate her meals through a straw while winking at inanimate objects. This did not stop her from pursuing a successful political career.*

Blake shot a look at Nicki, who was sadly shaking her head.

No luck on the trace.

'How am I supposed to break into GADO?' Blake asked Badde. 'It's one of the most secure facilities on Earth.'

'You're inventive. You'll think of a way.'

'Let me speak to Lisa.'

'All right, but I will insist on laughing in a really evil fashion when I sign off.'

Silence followed, then—

'Dad?'

The sound of her voice almost broke his heart. 'I'm coming for you, Lisa,' he said. 'I won't give up.'

'I know, Dad,' she said, swallowing. 'He's already forced me to watch two episodes!'

'No!'

'There's one where Bobby gets a zit—'

'No!'

'And another one where Cindy learns how to bake a sponge cake.'

Oh no, Blake thought. *Not the sponge cake episode!*

Badde's voice came back on the line. 'I'm giving you two days,' he said. 'In the meantime, we'll see how much little Lisa can take.'

He started to laugh. It was a helpless chuckle that grew into an out-of-control roar. He even did the horrible giggling thing that maniacs do, ending in a gurgle like something going down the drain.

The sound rang in Blake's ears long after Badde had hung up.

11

It took Blake a moment to realise Nicki was talking to him.

'I've tried tracing the call,' she was saying. 'I got as far as a pasta bar in Japan, but it was relayed through an insurance office in Hong Kong, bounced off a sheep station in Australia and then a taco joint on the moon.' She shook her head. 'I lost it after that.'

'Where was the phone purchased?'

'A delicatessen in Dubai.'

'They might have security cameras. But it's unlikely Badde would have made the purchase himself.' Blake shook his head. 'He's got Lisa.'

'What are you going to do?'

'Get her back. Which means I need to get into GADO.'

'What do you mean, *you* need to get into GADO?' Nicki said. 'I'm not a pencil sharpener. I'm your partner. That means we work together.'

Blake stared at Nicki. She had obviously short-circuited.

'Agent Steel,' he said, 'I appreciate the offer, but I'm talking about breaking into GADO, the most secure facility on Earth.'

'All the more reason you need me.'

'You know what you're saying? If we get caught, we'd be charged with treason. Our reputations would be ruined. And it's a mandatory life sentence.'

'That could be a problem for me,' Nicki admitted. 'Theoretically, I might live forever. You, on the other hand, are a short-lived lump of carbon with your best days behind you.'

'Thanks,' he said. 'I think.'

'So you've got two choices: you can include me on this assignment and dramatically increase your chances of success, or—'

'*Or?*'

'I contact the assistant director and tell him what you're planning. It's up to you.'

Blake rubbed his chin. Nicki was right. Having her along would turn an impossible mission into…well, a slightly less impossible mission. Two heads were probably better than one, even when the other was made from metal and plastic.

'Why do you want to help?' he asked. 'You barely know me.'

'It's how I'm programmed.'

'Don't blame me when you spend the next million years in jail.'

She shrugged. 'With good behaviour I could be out in half that time.'

Blake frowned. 'We just need to work out how to break in,' he said.

'I've already formulated several plans.'

'What?'

'Blake,' Nicki said, patiently, 'my brain is capable of twenty-four gazillion calculations per second.'

Zeeb says:

> *A gazillion is a really big number, but it's not the biggest. Even if you put a nine at the front, there is a bigger number and that number was first calculated on the planet Trian Four.*

> *It had long been rumoured that the Trians had discovered the largest number in existence within a deep cavern on their planet. An ancient civilisation known as the Gaarrggg (I think it's a silly name too, but people can call themselves whatever they want) had grown a giant mushroom to use as a calculating machine.*

> *Yes, a mushroom. The Gaarrggg had long since discarded synthetic materials and grew their computers from biological waste.*

When the Gaarrggg prime minister, Bastmuffin Gelda, confronted the mushroom, demanding to be told the largest number in existence, the mushroom asked, 'Are you sure you want to know?'

'Absolutely,' said Prime Minister Gelda.

'Really sure?'

'Definitely.'

'Are you positively certain—'

'Just tell me the sprottin' number!'

'Well, okay,' the mushroom said. 'It's—'

And it told him.

The prime minister stood, thoughtful, for about five minutes. Then the left side of his mouth began to twitch. Shortly after, his whole face started moving uncontrollably. Then his right eyeball popped out as he laughed and repeatedly punched himself in the jaw.

By the time his advisers checked to see how he was doing, they found him on the floor chewing his left foot.

The whole incident was all rather unexpected. The mushroom, meanwhile, had said nothing more, and sat in the cave, looking rather pleased with itself.

'What the sprot happened?' the deputy prime minister asked. 'What went wrong?'

'I told him the largest number in existence,' replied the mushroom.

'Which was?'

Not really a very clever thing to ask, because the mushroom told her. Some hours later they found the deputy prime minister sitting alone on the floor of the cave with Prime Minister Gelda's right arm poking out from her mouth. No one was sure what had happened to Gelda until they realised most of him was now inside the deputy prime minister.

It was quite a disappointing result all round, and the cave was sealed up shortly afterwards. I've often wondered what happened to that mushroom. Did they cook and eat it? Personally, I like mushrooms with a little butter and—

'How many plans have you come up with?' Blake asked.

'Twelve,' Nicki said. 'However, I would rate nine of them as nothing short of suicidal. And our chances of succeeding in two of the others are no better than surviving a jump off the mile-high Wobontom Tower— without a parachute.'

'And the remaining plan?'

'Still not great odds,' Nicki admitted. 'We would need help from someone who's good with a jet pack.'

'You mean,' Blake said, 'a scarmish jet pack?'

'That would do.'

Sprot.

12

Astrid Carter was worried sick. Lisa still hadn't come home.

Astrid had rung the police, but they had said a missing person's report couldn't be filed until two days had passed. Then they had suggested that Lisa might have run away, so Astrid had angrily hung up on them.

Lisa wouldn't run away, she thought. *But where is she?*

It wasn't like her daughter to go off without telling her. They had planned to go out and get their hair cut; a great new salon had opened on level 800. And besides, Lisa had no reason to leave. She was perfectly happy at home. Wasn't she?

Astrid stared gloomily out her living room window. They lived on the 600th level on the north side in a nice apartment. It had a view of a park, which was pleasant, as far as high-rise parks go, with trees, shrubs, flowers and a grassy lawn. They were all synthetic, but so was everything these days.

A bubbling stream, lined by benches, ran through the park. On one of the benches was a plaque that paid tribute to the ancient indigenous people who had once lived in the region, albeit several hundred feet below.

Zeeb says:

> *Sadly, there is little else to mark the end of their grand civilisation. If archaeologists were to dig under Astrid's building, they would find stone tips from their arrows and markings on a cave wall. Under that layer of civilisation they would find a plastic rhino from a 21st-century time-travel experiment, and twenty feet below that a crashed spaceship from the planet Xanthros.*

I've got to ring Blake again, Astrid thought. *He knows people, and can make things happen.*

It had been strange speaking to him yesterday. Unlike Lisa, she bore him no ill will. What was done was done, and they all had to get on with their lives.

What would he think of the apartment? The carpet was different, decorated with a print of Yuri Gagarin's helmeted head. A television screen covered the whole west side of the living room, with family picture vids on the other side. They made the place seem like a typical family home, even though one member was conspicuously absent.

Books—ones made from paper—covered another wall. As a literature professor for the 99th Block University, Astrid had been teaching for years. The students were always amazed when she pulled an antique book from her bag. Most of them had never seen one.

Astrid glanced at herself in the mirror. Her hair was still black, her curves more or less intact, and her eyes still olive, unlike most people these days who were getting their irises changed monthly.

The front door sneezed. The sneezing door was not her idea. It had come fitted with a variety of sound effects: sneezing, farting, wheezing, screaming, laughing, crying, giggling. Astrid was an old-fashioned girl. A simple *ding-dong* would have sufficed, but kids always wanted the latest and greatest.

'*Ah-choo!*'

She hurried to the door, expecting to find her daughter wearing a sheepish expression. Instead, she found her ex-husband and a rather attractive-looking golden robot.

Her heart leapt into her throat.

Zeeb says:
   No, her heart did not really leap into her throat. That's just a cliché, which is a way for a writer to avoid being original.

Interestingly, a weapon on Diondrax Major was actually designed to make your heart leap into your throat, which is a rather nasty thing to do to someone. One minute you're racing across a battlefield, the next instant your anatomy has been rearranged so that one of your vital organs is blocking your windpipe.

As methods of dying go, this is one of the more gruesome, and it makes me wonder why people can't do more worthwhile things with their time. Painting, for example, or stamp-collecting.

'No,' she muttered. 'Is it…?'

Suddenly the strength went from Astrid's legs and she fell against the doorframe.

'Lisa is okay,' Blake said, grabbing her arm. 'At least, for now. Can we come in?'

They followed Astrid into the living room, where she folded her arms and glared at them. The robot's blue eyes were disconcerting, as if something were alive in there other than chips and circuits.

'What the hell is going on, Blake?'

He explained about Badde and his theft of the Super-EMP, and then Lisa's kidnapping. Astrid listened in silence. She did not interrupt. She did not yell. She did not dredge up their past.

She did, however, punch Blake in the face.

Before she could do it again, Nicki forced her down onto the lounge. 'I can understand you wanting to kill him,' she said, 'and I've only known him for a day. But this isn't Blake's fault.'

Fighting back angry tears, Astrid scowled at him. 'It's always Blake's fault!' she snapped. 'He's always rubbing people the wrong way!'

Zeeb says:

They have some rather odd expressions on Earth. 'Rubbing' someone or something 'the wrong way' is just one of them. Another is the expression 'having a Gladys', named after Gladys Olsen, who lived in what used to be Renshaw, Nebraska. Gladys became known as the unluckiest person on Earth.

While walking to school at the age of seven, Gladys was hit on the head by a falling meteorite and knocked senseless. But this was just the start of her troubles. At fifteen, she was struck by lightning. When she was nineteen, a falling tree branch broke her left arm.

By the age of thirty, Gladys had ended up in hospital on no less than thirty-seven separate occasions.

Possibly the most bizarre incident involved a stampede of gazelles as Gladys strolled to church. How the gazelles came to be charging down a back street in Renshaw, Nebraska, has never been established, but she broke both legs in the incident.

Finally, a television program called Lucky to Survive *decided to give Gladys an award as recognition for her extraordinary run of bad luck.*

*Stepping onto the stage to accept the award she
began, 'I just want to thank the producers—'*

*Which was as far as she got. A long defunct
satellite happened to fall from the sky at that
moment, killing her instantly. The only part of her
body recovered from the scene was her left hand.*

*To this day, there are still left hands being sold
on gBay as good luck charms, all claiming to be
the real deal. I doubt their authenticity. The one I
bought certainly hasn't done me any good.*

'Nicki's right,' Blake said. 'And we need to focus on saving Lisa.'

'You haven't rung the authorities?' Astrid asked.

'We *are* the authorities,' Blake reminded her. 'And Badde made it clear we'd never see Lisa again if we brought in the department.'

'So what do we do?'

'We've got a plan. Or Nicki does.'

'The robot?' Astrid said, eyeing her sceptically. 'You do more than play chess and vacuum under lounges?'

'I'm a cyborg,' Nicki said, more patiently than she was feeling. She glanced around the room, her eyes settling on a picture vid of Astrid competing in the 2493 Interplanetary Scarmish Final. 'I have a way to get us into GADO, but we'll need your help.'

'What do I have to do?'

Blake leant forward. 'Do you still have your old scarmish gear?' he asked.

13

Milton Xanthrob was surprised when the doorbell tinkled and three people walked into his shop. Perkins Antiques was located on the 336th level of Neo City's south side, far away from most foot traffic, and customers were rare.

It was early and the street outside was dark. There was only artificial lighting down here, and mostly it didn't work too well. An odd fungus had started to grow in the crevices of the buildings. Milton had lived here for so long he half expected it to start growing on him, but he didn't mind. His life was simple, and if he had to contend with a little mould, well, so be it.

During the day, he would sit behind the counter, reading and watching TV, whiling away the hours till closing time. Dying here was a very real possibility—and that was fine, too. Everything had a time and a place, and he'd had an exceptionally happy life.

How Milton had ended up owning the shop was a story in itself. He had gone to Perkins Antiques to get a clock valued. It was an unusual Art Deco piece, still working, with the face showing the correct time and date, but the switches on the back were stuck in place.

The previous owner of the shop had been an elderly man by the name of Bruce Perkins. The clock looked unusual to him too. He thought if he could get the switches working he might be able to work out their function. Perkins sat at his counter, applied some oil to them, struggled to move one—and abruptly broke the universe.

Or so it seemed to Milton at the time.

A fuzzy hole appeared on the countertop. Perkins opened his mouth to speak, but before he could utter a word both he and his counter started to *bleed* into the hole. Milton leapt back in horror.

Sprot!

The hole shrank. Milton Xanthrob stared open-mouthed into the diminishing gap. It was like looking into a tunnel. Beyond it was a tube of inky blackness ending in a smaller circle of light.

Peering at that faraway glow, Milton thought he could see patches of green vegetation and the distant counter. Behind it, Perkins was yelling. Milton made out the words 'dinosaur' and 'tyrannosaurus' before the hole disappeared.

The shop, smelling of ozone, was otherwise unchanged, barring the missing owner and counter. Milton stood there, alone and afraid, expecting to be arrested at any moment. He had, after all, been partially responsible for the disappearance of Bruce Perkins.

But nothing happened. The police did not appear. Nobody dragged Milton away to jail. Finally, he sat down on Mr Perkins' chair until his legs stopped shaking.

An hour later a customer walked in, picked out an old vase and insisted on giving money to Milton. After some hesitation, he accepted the cash and the customer walked away a happy man.

It took him a few days, but Milton discovered both he and Perkins had a lot in common: they both loved antiques and had no family. By the end of the week Milton had purchased a new counter and hung a sign in the window for anyone who happened to be passing.

Under New Management.

That was twenty years ago. He still had in his possession an article he'd found in a magazine called *Strange But True*. In it was a story about a fossilised human skull wearing a pair of glasses that had been found in Arizona. Readers were invited to write in with theories regarding the bizarre discovery.

Milton, deciding that discretion was the better part of valour, did not contribute.

The people who walked into Milton's shop on this particular day were an odd trio. The man, wearing an old trench coat, was so dishevelled Milton assumed he was a hobo. The robot woman was stunning, and could have passed for human except for the gold skin. The other woman was also good-looking, but her face had creased into a worried frown. They all wore backpacks.

After spending some time perusing the shop, they finally approached the counter. The hobo cleared his throat. 'We'd like to dig a hole through the back of your shop,' he said. 'Not a big hole. Just large enough for us to fit through.'

Milton Xanthrob stared at him.

'My ex-husband phrased that rather badly,' the woman said, clearly embarrassed. 'We'd like to give you some money to leave the shop for the day.'

'Think of it as a holiday,' the robot added.

'Yes, that's it,' the ex-wife said. 'A holiday. Somewhere you haven't been before.'

'We'll look after your shop while you're away,' the hobo said.

Silence.

'This doesn't have anything to do with Mr Perkins?' Milton asked.

The strangers exchanged glances.

'Who?'

'Never mind,' Milton said. 'Uh, where do you suggest I go?'

'Oh, anywhere,' the man said airily. 'The moon is rather pleasant this time of year.'

Zeeb says:

> *Blake Carter may be a very good detective, but this is one of the most stupid things you will read in this book. Despite all the facilities that now exist there, including the new Lunar Disney resort, the moon is not a pleasant place to visit. A trip there makes watching Cybardian paint dry look like an action sport—and Cybardian paint takes over a century to dry.*
>
> *The moon is dull. Dull, dull, dull. Truly it is one of the dullest places in the whole galaxy. Venus is far more pleasant, and you can get a package deal if you go mid-season.*

'Or Mars,' the robot suggested. 'Mars is nice.'

'Here's some money.' The ex-wife reached into her pocket and pulled out a plastic card. 'Spend some.'

Milton Xanthrob nervously made his way to the door.

'We'll look after the store,' the robot promised.

'Everything's priced,' Milton said. 'Just hand out a receipt.' He appeared thoughtful. 'I might go to the moon.'

Zeeb says:

> *Which is probably the second most stupid thing you'll read in this book...*

'That was easier than I expected,' Blake said, breathing a sigh of relief after Milton left.

'Poor man,' Astrid said. 'Mustn't get out much.'

'We're probably doing him a favour,' Nicki said.

'Except for the hole in his wall,' Blake said.

They went to a storage room in the back where they found a kitchenette and rows of shelves stacked with antiques.

'This looks pretty organised,' Astrid said.

'It does,' Nicki agreed, grabbing a shelf, pulling it over and destroying a thousand years of history.

'Nicki!' Blake yelled. 'What the sprot are you doing?'

'Was that stuff valuable?'

'That little man is going to hate us,' Astrid said.

'I've been hated before,' Nicki said. 'I survived.'

Blake rapped on the wall. 'You're sure this is where we go through?' he asked Nicki.

'Definitely. Beyond this wall lies a disused elevator that'll take us down to a tunnel. We can follow that all the way to a cavern under the GADO complex.'

'I wonder how we should break through.'

Nicki pushed back her hair. 'Fortunately,' she said, 'I'm trained in twenty-two different forms of martial arts.'

'So?' Astrid frowned.

'I can generate a one-inch punch that will easily knock a hole in the wall.'

'We could also just use our blasters,' Blake said. 'A single shot at high intensity—'

'And rob me of the opportunity to show off?' Nicki said. 'No way.'

She drew her right arm back, focused, took a deep breath and slammed her fist into the wall. A torrent of water burst through the gap, knocking Nicki over and demolishing another shelf.

'Hmm,' Nicki said, pushing debris aside. 'I wasn't expecting that.'

Zeeb says:

Strangely, this expression has been used many times over the centuries, mostly by people of science. Faraday used it when he discovered electromagnetic induction, Archimedes when he overflowed his bath and Marju Rastor said it when he invented the quantum drive.

One of the more unfortunate times these words were uttered came about when Janck Ontono discovered material transmutation. The Mantaris scientist had been struggling for decades to find a way to turn one object into another.

On this particular day, he was attempting to turn an apple into a lemon. The apple had been sitting in his multi-nucleonic transmutation device for over an hour with nothing happening. Finally, he made a minor adjustment to the radioactive bombardment, and something strange started to occur.

Something very strange.

Everything began to take on a yellow hue. Not just the apple—everything. Including the transmutation device, Ontono himself, and the room around him.

'I wasn't expecting that,' he murmured.

A second later, the planet Mantaris turned into an enormous lemon floating in space. There was even a green bit sticking out from where the planet's north pole used to be.

This was all very unfortunate for two reasons. First, 'I wasn't expecting that' are not great famous last words for a ten-million-year-old civilisation. And second, while it's really wonderful to be handed a lemon in life and turn it into lemonade, you really need a planet to do it.

'Nicki!' Blake yelled as more water spurted through the hole. 'I thought you said the tunnel was behind here?'

'I did,' she replied. 'I don't think this is the right wall.' She spent the next few minutes pulling over shelves and punching holes in walls before turning to the others and yelling, 'I've found it! The elevator shaft is here!'

'Great,' Astrid said nervously.

While Nicki made the hole bigger so they could climb through, Astrid glanced back to the shop behind them. It did not look very much like the organised little storeroom they had entered only a few minutes earlier. Most of what had been on the shelves was now swimming in a foot of water.

They climbed through the hole onto the top of an elevator and lowered themselves through a roof hatch into the compartment.

'There's only two buttons,' Astrid said. 'Up and down.'

'Down it is,' Blake said.

He hit the button. For a moment, nothing happened.

Then they dropped like a rock.

14

Blake had always heard about people's lives flashing before their eyes when faced with death.

This did not happen.

What he did see was a close-up of Astrid's ankle because, with the three of them plastered against the ceiling, her foot was in his face. He wanted to say something prophetic or heroic to her, but nothing came to mind. He was busy screaming along with the others as the elevator plummeted faster than a spaceship caught in the gravity pull of a black hole.

Finally they slowed, crashing in an untidy heap on the floor.

'That was rougher than I expected,' Astrid said,

dusting herself off. 'Almost as bad as Blake's driving.'

'My driving's not so bad,' Blake said. 'Once you get used to it.'

'If you survive long enough.'

The elevator doors slid open to reveal two astonished men on the other side.

'You're here!' one cried. 'Finally!'

'We've waited so long,' the other gasped, tears in his eyes. 'I'll get Gastanon.'

'Where are we?' Blake asked.

As the second man disappeared down the corridor, the first gave them a gentle smile. 'Ah, we know the prophets have a sense of humour,' he said. 'It is only that sense of humour that has kept us going all these years. Welcome to—Perfection.'

'Really?' Blake peered down the corridor. It didn't look like perfection. It looked like a rather dank and gloomy corridor. 'And who do you think we are?'

'Another joke,' the man said, laughing. 'It makes the waiting more worthwhile.'

They followed him down the tunnel to a cavern the size of several football fields. It was packed with trees and plants, growing everything from apples to pumpkins to oranges. Hydroponic lights hung from the ceiling, bathing the crops in a bright, clean glow. Men and women dressed in plain grey shirts and pants toiled in the fields.

Painted in huge letters across one wall were the words: *They will return.*

'What is this place?' Astrid whispered to Blake.

'It's…Perfection, whatever that is.'

'Whoever they are,' Nicki said, 'they've been here a long time.' She pointed. 'Those lights are Eterno bulbs, designed more than two hundred years ago. They never burn out, which is why the company went out of business.'

They were led to a house where people gazed at them in reverence and amazement. A lean man wearing a goatee cautiously approached.

'I am Gastanon,' he introduced himself. 'And who is Hysteronomous? And Pythergonius and Slyvanathium?'

'Huh?' Blake said.

'Which of you is which?' Gastanon asked.

Blake, Nicki and Astrid stared at him.

'I think you've got us mixed up with someone else,' Blake finally said. 'We're not any kind of prophets. We're from above.'

'From the Promised Land,' Gastanon said, nodding with satisfaction. 'We know. It lies beyond the world of ultimate devastation.'

'Which world of ultimate devastation are you referring to?' Astrid asked. 'Devastation is a bit rough, even for Detroit.'

Gastanon laughed. 'You are testing us,' he said. 'Stories have been passed down to us about the tests.'

'That's right,' Astrid said, deciding it was easier to play along. 'We're testing you. Now tell us what all this is about.'

'Of course. But first we must go to the place of speaking so that all may know the truth.'

They followed Gastanon to a citadel in the middle of the fields, and climbed steps to a podium. Crowds had gathered. There had to be over ten thousand people here.

Gastanon stepped up to the microphone.

'Is this thing on?' he asked, tapping it. 'Can you hear me down the back?' A bunch of people yelled in the affirmative. 'Wonderful. You have no doubt heard the exciting news—the Prophets have returned!'

The crowd went wild with excitement, cheering and clapping. The sound of their applause echoed about the interior of the cavern.

'As you know,' Gastanon continued, 'the Prophets work in mysterious ways. They want us to relate our history before we begin our Ascension.'

'The Dummies guide would be good,' Nicki added.

Gastanon smiled serenely. 'It began with the great cleansing, the war that devastated the surface of the Earth, leaving it uninhabitable for a million years. We, the Survivors, had already built our underground world knowing that humanity would soon face total annihilation.'

'Who told you to do this?' Nicki interrupted.

Gastanon laughed. 'You are jesting, of course.'

'Yeah, I'm jesting. I've never jested so much in my entire life. Now just tell me whose bright idea this was.'

'The great Quasido Smith, of course. Our founder, our hero, the man who saved us from utter devastation.'

Taking out her datapad, Nicki started tapping keys.

'Our ancestors gave up everything to come down here,' Gastanon continued. 'They carved this cavern with their bare hands. They starved so that the first crops would grow. They ruthlessly slaughtered the weakest citizens to make way for the strong. They fought tooth and nail to build a new world.

'But build it they did. After facing starvation, conflict, internal strife and a really bad flea infestation, they finally built the ultimate community—Perfection.'

'And where did you put it?' Astrid asked, peering about into the distance.

'Pardon?'

'Where is it?'

'Why, here, of course,' Gastanon said. 'This is Perfection.'

'Oh.'

'We have lived in complete harmony since those dark early days,' Gastanon continued. 'Crime is extinct and war is over. For more than a century there has been only peace.' He paused. 'But we have waited.'

'I know the feeling,' Blake muttered.

'Quasido Smith said that one day the Prophets would arrive to lead us to the Promised Land,' he said. 'Now that day has arrived!'

The crowd went wild again. Many wept with joy. Some fell to their knees, thumping their chests. A couple went into convulsions.

'Take us!' one yelled. 'Take us to the Promised Land!'

Another called, 'When will we go?'

'I want to see our ancestors!' a man screamed. 'Have they been asking about me?'

Gastanon stepped aside and indicated that Blake should take the microphone. Slowly, Blake inched towards it, clearing his throat.

'Uh,' he said. 'Hello.'

It took another five minutes to calm down the crowd.

'So,' Blake said, finally. 'I've got some good news.'

'Tell us the good news!' the crowd screamed.

'Well, you see, it's like this…'

Nicki motioned Blake out of the way. 'What Blake's trying to say is that there was no war. The human race didn't go extinct. It's chugging along fine, if you ignore the pollution, famine, overcrowding and politicians.'

The crowd stared at her.

'There's good stuff up there,' she said. 'You can travel to other planets, meet aliens from a thousand different worlds and explore unknown space.' She paused. 'Or if you want to stay on Earth, there are 2000 types of flavoured ice-cream, 24,000,000 television channels and food from all over the galaxy.' She shrugged. 'It's kind of cool.'

Gastanon's face had fallen. 'You're jesting, of course,' he said. 'The surface is devastated. Nothing can live up there.'

'There are places like that,' Astrid conceded. 'Some of the McBurger restaurants are really unhygienic… Believe me, you don't want to go there.'

Nicki nodded in earnest agreement. 'But mostly it's fine,' she said. 'I did a search on Quasido Smith. He was the guy who told you to live in this hole? Right?'

'Yes,' Gastanon said, crestfallen.

'Turns out he was picked up for fraud in 2281 and jailed for ninety-nine years. Seems he had this scam where he convinced people the world was coming to an end. They would give him all their worldly possessions in exchange for a way to survive the apocalypse.' Nicki sighed. 'It sounds like your ancestors got taken for a ride.'

'A...ride.'

'Yeah,' Blake said, nodding thoughtfully. 'I remember reading about Quasido Smith in the PBI history books. He was a real scammer.'

Zeeb says:

> *Quasido Smith was in fact so completely without conscience that he once wheedled his own mother out of her life savings, and left her at a bus station in Portland, Oregon, never to return.*

> *Over the course of his career, he ran every kind of scam you can imagine. His speciality in the early days was selling the Brooklyn Bridge. So many people eventually believed they were the rightful owners of the bridge that a brawl erupted on the bridge during a public meeting. The bridge was destroyed in the ensuing battle.*

> *Smith moved on to bigger and better things, selling moons, planets and even a few stars.*

On the run from the authorities, he started inventing his own religions. These hinged on the fact that doomsday was around the corner and only one person held the key to salvation—Quasido Smith.

'So,' Nicki said, trying to make sense of all this, 'your ancestors moved down here because…?'

'Quasido Smith said it would save us,' Gastanon said, 'from the end of the world.'

'Well,' Astrid said. 'You must be pleased that the world still exists.'

Still exists.

The words echoed around the interior of the cavern.

Gastanon spoke slowly, struggling to piece together the puzzle. 'You're saying Quasido Smith was a conman and everything is fine up above.'

'I wouldn't exactly say fine,' Blake said.

'Oh,' Gastanon said, looking relieved.

'But pretty good.'

Nicki and Astrid agreed.

'You're saying everything is okay.' Gastanon looked out at the crowd in dismay. 'We've slaved away for two centuries to build Perfection and you're saying it's built on a lie. That the deprivation, pain, humiliation and daily torment we've suffered is…okay?'

'Um…well…' Blake said.

Astrid chimed up. 'You should be proud of yourselves,' she said. 'You're living here in peace and harmony. You're living here in…Perfection.'

'Perfection?' Gastanon's face twitched. 'We're living in a hole in the ground. A dirty, grubby underground bunker.' He spun around, wildly. 'Do you know how many people I've wanted to punch in the face?' He pointed at a man in the audience. 'Starting with you!' He picked up the microphone stand and hurled it. 'You never take out the rubbish on time—and I'm sick of it!'

The microphone stand hit the stranger in the head and rebounded into someone else's face. They punched someone who had nothing to do with anything. Another person grabbed the stand and started stabbing people at random.

'Kill you!' Gastanon screamed. 'I'm going to kill—'

Whatever else he had to say was stifled as he leapt into the crowd.

Within seconds the audience was involved in the biggest brawl since the riots of 2309. Knives were produced, gardening implements were raised and axes thrown. Blood and body parts began to fly.

'I think we should go,' Blake said.

'No arguments here,' Astrid said.

They pushed through the crowd, carving their way to an exit. Within minutes they had reached the elevator, where Nicki made a pleasant discovery.

'Look,' she said, pointing down. 'There's a button with a sign above it.'

'What's it say?' Blake asked.

'*Push to reinitialise elevator.*'

She pushed the button, the doors opened wide and they slipped in. The sound of screaming and fighting died away as the doors slid shut.

Nicki shook her head. 'Eternal peace,' she said, as she pushed *Up*. 'It never lasts.'

15

'What do you want *now*?' Bartholomew Badde asked.

'A Game Prism would be a good start,' Lisa said. 'And a bag of bacon-flavoured chips. Oh, and a bottle of Hypergo.'

'You're too young to be drinking Hypergo.'

'Who are you? My mother?'

'I'm just saying—'

'And it's *waaay* too dark in here,' Lisa said, peering about. 'Really unpleasant.'

The jail looked like something from olden times. Maybe even ancient Rome. The cell had only one window—a small, barred frame set high on the other side of the room—and contained a bunk bed and a chair.

The only modern thing in the room, unfortunately, was the triple-digitised combination lock attached to the bars. Lisa thought she could crack it if she tried every single combination, but that would probably take about 7,000,000 years.

Badde himself was thin and bald, with a neat black moustache. The wrinkles around his eyes made him look like he was sixty, but he moved like a man half that age. He wore a plain grey suit, white button-down shirt and black shoes.

'It's supposed to be unpleasant,' Badde said. 'You're a hostage, and I'm the greatest diabolical genius in history, responsible for crimes across the galaxy. My name will go down in history with—'

'Yeah, yeah,' Lisa said. 'Yada, yada, yada.'

'Yada—what?'

'Yada—as in, I've heard it all before.'

'What do you mean?'

'Evil criminal geniuses are always doing nasty things. That's how they're programmed.'

'But I am the *most* evil genius in history.'

'I know, and it's nice to have goals, but you need to be ready for when things go wrong.'

'Things won't go wrong.'

'That's what they all say,' Lisa said, patiently. 'But there's always that part of the movie where the evil genius says, "Okay, Mr Jones, I've got to leave now to bake some cookies while you're slowly lowered into a vat of bubbling acid." The villain leaves, and the hero uses his absence to escape.'

'But your name isn't Jones and I don't have a vat of bubbling acid,' Badde said, frowning. 'Mind you, it's not a bad idea...'

'But you see what I mean,' Lisa said. 'And besides, you don't want damaged goods.'

'I don't?'

'I'm worth money. Lots of money. But hostage negotiations can take forever. I might be here for years.'

'You won't be here for years. Once I get those *Brady Bunch* episodes underway—'

'I'll admit they're pretty revolting,' Lisa said. It was in fact the worst television show she'd ever seen. 'But don't you know a happy hostage is a compliant hostage?'

Badde considered this. 'I suppose I can turn on the lights,' he said. 'That's easy.'

'And I need Chuckie's Chicken.'

'Whose chicken?'

Lisa Carter looked at Badde as if he'd grown a second head.

Zeeb says:

You may have seen my documentary, The Spontaneous Generation of Second Heads on Delorius Prime. *The whole issue is really quite disconcerting. It makes you wonder why anyone lives there. One second you're eating breakfast with your partner, the next they have another head protruding from their shoulder.*

No one has ever come up with an explanation for the heads, who have no memory of previous lives. Most are quite pleasant, however, working with their newly acquired bodies to make Delorius Prime a better world, proving that two heads really are better than one.

'You've never heard of Chuckie's Chicken!' Lisa exclaimed. 'Where have you been living?'

Badde folded his arms. 'I've been busy.'

'Doing what?'

'Oh, the usual evil things. Robberies, forgeries assaults.'

Lisa sighed. 'Anyway, I'll have the Chuckie Two Pack with chips,' she said. 'Extra chocolate salt on the chips, and don't forget my bottle of Hypergo.'

When Badde left, Lisa stood in the centre of the cell for another moment before carefully stepping backwards and falling onto her bed.

At last. Now she could relax.

Despite her bravado, her heart had been pounding the whole time she was talking to Badde. She had gotten the upper hand—for now—but she wasn't sure how long that would last. It looked like he had turned nasty into an art form.

And I'm his canvas, she thought.

Lisa's heart eventually stopped thudding. The room had gone quiet, apart from the occasional wheeze of an interplanetary shuttle passing by, or the shudder of an orbital lift carrying people into space. Both were close by, but they gave no clue as to her location.

She had been walking home from the 704th level Super-Mall when a shadowy figure had stepped from a dark alley and shot her with a stun gun. Her next conscious thought had been when she woke up in this mangy cell with a killer headache.

'Sprot,' she said. 'And double sprot.'

According to Badde, her father had to retrieve the Maria virus or she would be made to pay. Lisa wondered how he was doing. She had not spoken to him in years, but once or twice she thought she'd spotted him lurking outside her school. Not talking to him all this time had hurt her, but she hurt even more when she thought about her birthday party.

It had been the most embarrassing day of her life. She had promised all the girls that he was going to make an amazing appearance—maybe skydiving in from the edge of space or teleporting into the middle of the living room. Instead he had surprised her by not turning up at all.

She'd mostly become used to being disappointed. After all, how many times could someone be let down before it became second nature? But Lisa couldn't forget the look on Martha Farnworth's face. The girl's family was made of *old* money, earned seven centuries before by an ancestor who had owned a thimble factory.

'Maybe your dad had to work,' Martha had suggested. 'There are lots of people who still do that.'

Martha wasn't being intentionally cruel. She had looked concerned.

And that *hurt*.

Today Lisa had realised something she had forgotten. Despite his many failings, she still loved her father.

The cell seemed to close in around her. She tried to quell the quaking in her stomach. Her parents weren't the sort to sit back and do nothing, and neither was she.

Bartholomew Badde might think he has the upper hand, she thought. *But he doesn't know what he's letting himself in for.*

16

Blake marvelled at his own stupidity. He had successfully landed himself in yet another dark and smelly place.

Why does this always happen to me?

This dark and smelly place, like so many others, was filled with strange sounds. They were made by rats—or Blake hoped they were.

The elevator had deposited the three of them in a tunnel that Nicki had quickly confirmed led to the Global Arms Defence Organisation. It had been a relief at first to be away from Perfection, but now Blake had the unpleasant feeling they were being followed.

He shone the torch behind them, cutting the gloom like a laser. The large tunnel had railway tracks, and disused pipes along the walls. It was obvious no one had been down here for years. Maybe centuries.

'What is it?' Astrid asked.

'Just checking,' Blake said.

'Like hell. What's back there?'

They all peered into the distance, a wall of solid black far beyond the range of the torch.

'I can't see anything,' Blake said.

'Me neither,' Astrid said.

'My eyes, despite their radiant beauty,' Nicki said, 'can't make out anything either, though I can check my other sensors.'

As she held out an arm, a patch of golden skin slid sideways and a radar dish popped out. It spun around, beeped a few times and rapidly snapped back out of sight.

'Hmm,' she said, 'that's a worry. I'm getting unusually high levels of radiation.'

'Radiation?' Astrid said. 'What's that?'

'Back in the 20th century,' Nicki explained, 'primitive humans had a brief and unsuccessful flirtation with nuclear energy.'

'What sort of idiots were they?'

'Well, on the Hopkins Chart of Idiot Behaviour, they ranked—'

'Never mind,' Blake interrupted. 'Just tell us if we're in any danger?'

'That depends on your definition of *we*,' Nicki said. 'My deutronium skin is virtually indestructible, so I could live down here for centuries with no ill effects.'

'And what about us?'

'You'll be fine, just as long as you don't mind losing all your hair, your teeth falling out, and ending up looking like a prune—'

'How long have we got?'

'Your organs will suffer irreparable damage in about an hour,' Nicki said. 'After that you will both be reduced to melted bags of glow-in-the-dark goo.'

'What a relief,' Astrid said. 'I thought we might be in trouble.'

'My map shows that this tunnel reaches a junction in about a mile. The walls are reinforced there and should protect us.'

'Then we'd better hurry,' Blake said.

Doubling their speed, they rushed down the tunnel. They didn't see the creature slithering after them. It had existed quite happily for hundreds of years without interference. But now it had been disturbed—and it didn't like it.

Where it came from, or how it had come into being, was beyond the creature's comprehension. All it knew was that it did not exist and then it did. There was the *before* and there was the *after*. Of the before, it knew nothing. In the after, it found itself surrounded by cold, moist blackness. Over time, it gradually came to realise that other living things also inhabited this strange ecosystem.

It also knew it was hungry.

Mostly, the creature was satisfied by a diet of rats and passing cockroaches. Once, many years before, a stray dog had fallen down an ancient ventilation shaft, landing only a few feet away.

The dog's name was Casper and he had broken one of his legs. Whimpering, he had limped about in the dark. There was a strange smell down here, Casper thought. *A cheesy smell.*

Then Casper stepped onto something spongy and warm. Before he could react, Casper was abruptly folded in half, chopped into multiple pieces, sucked down a six-inch digestive tract and reduced to acidic sludge.

Zeeb says:
  Did I mention there'd be yucky bits?

The creature still remembered the taste of the dog, often recalling its demise with great pleasure. Or what passed for pleasure. It remembered the myriad scents it had picked up from the dog before its death—strange, tantalising odours that teased it with hints of another world.

The creature had often wondered about that world.

Today, some of it had intruded into its domain.

It had begun with:

Clang. Clang. Clang.

Then—

'You're on my foot!'

'You weigh a ton!'

'Get off my hand!'

The sounds had meant little to the creature, but the scents had piqued its interest. One of the newcomers held no more appeal than a brick, but the other two were positively...desirable. They could be its best meal in two centuries.

'Garrrfffff,' it said.

The cry carried down the long tunnel to where Blake had just climbed over a rockfall where the ceiling had collapsed.

'Did you hear that?'

'I did,' Nicki said. 'I think we're being followed.'

'By what?' Blake asked.

'Well, it's a thing.'

'A *thing*?' Blake stared at her. 'An IQ of 30,000,000 and the best you can come up with is *It's a thing*?'

'Okay.' Nicki paused. 'It's a really *big* thing.'

'Let's just get moving,' Astrid said. 'Whatever it is, we should keep our distance.'

They hurried down the tunnel, but the sound of slithering, accompanied by a wheezing growl, grew closer.

'We haven't known each other long,' Nicki said to the others. 'But I've grown quite fond of you.'

'Thank you, Nicki,' Astrid said.

'I'd hate to see you devoured by an underground monster.'

'Nice of you to say,' Blake said.

'To see you torn limb from limb,' Nicki continued. 'To see your eyes sucked from their sockets, to see your headless corpses—'

'We get the idea.'

'Uh oh,' Astrid said.

'Uh oh—what?' Blake asked.

But in the next instant he knew. The tunnel abruptly ended at a concrete wall.

'What the sprot is this?' Blake said.

'Oh dear,' Nicki said. 'The maps haven't been updated.'

Zeeb says:

> *This is not unusual in Neo City. Possibly the most bizarre case of poor planning by the Neo City Council occurred when they fought for three years to have an old building demolished, only to discover it was its own council building.*
>
> *Only a flurry of last-minute letters submitted in triplicate, a petition signed by 1,000,000 voters and a personal plea from the Earth's president saved it from demolition.*

'I think it's a sewerage pipe,' Nicki said. 'Breaking through would flood the tunnel. I'd be fine, but those of us who need oxygen would have problems.'

Another growl rolled down the tunnel from behind.

'That sounds closer,' Astrid said.

'It is.' Nicki studied her datapad. 'This is interesting. The thing, uh, the really *big* thing, is a result of radioactive waste.' She did a double take. 'That's very odd.'

Before Nicki could define *very odd*, Astrid raised a shaking arm and pointed to the rockfall they had crossed only a minute before. Something had filled the gap above it.

Something dark. Something large.

The creature slithered resolutely over the obstacle, raised what passed for a head and sniffed the air with what could optimistically be called a nose.

Blake froze. Would their blasters work on the creature?

He made a tiny hand motion to the others to remain still. Maybe if the creature didn't see them, it would assume it had lost its prey and slither back to whatever hellhole it called home. Its 'head' moved about like a slug testing the air.

The creature seemed frustrated, as if sensing it had lost the trail, and slowly began to turn around.

It's working! Blake thought. *It's—*

'Yippee!' Nicki screamed. 'Come and get us, *you sprot eater*!'

The creature roared and then charged.

17

Barnaby Hazleton loved art.

His mother had taken him to the Louvre when he was a child and he had literally jumped for joy as she led him from room to room. As far as he was concerned, science helped you to live, but art gave you a reason *to* live.

Fortunately, his mother was a wealthy woman, allowing Barnaby to pursue his passion. As soon as he was old enough to pick up a paintbrush, he started producing his own paintings. He worked day and night, studying under the best art teachers Earth had to offer. But by the time of his twenty-first birthday, he had to face the terrible truth.

He had no artistic talent.

Oh, he could copy. He could reproduce Leonardo's *Mona Lisa* or Bargetti's *Seven Drapnas Eating the Mayor of Fellshaw* as accurately as a photograph. More accurately, some would say. His own teachers marvelled at how he could reproduce not only every brushstroke of the original artist but a sense of the artist as well. His teachers all agreed he was a marvellous copier, but as far as being able to *create* original work...

'Some of us have it,' Señor Felipe, his favourite teacher, told him one day. 'And some of us do not. Your composition is unbalanced. Your colours are wrong. Your tonal gradients...' He shuddered in silent horror. 'Well, you understand what I mean.'

'But surely I can improve!'

Señor Felipe had tried to be encouraging. 'Stick to what you are best at,' he said. 'Copying.'

This evaluation was so soul-destroying that Barnaby had given up art for a year. By this stage his mother had moved them to Neo City, purchasing an enormous underground apartment on the east side of town. Unfortunately, as her age increased, so did her eating, and by sixty she weighed over 400 pounds. Barnaby, meanwhile, remained in his room, gloomily watching soap operas and nature documentaries.

> *Zeeb says:*
> *This is not to say that there's anything wrong in watching nature documentaries. I encourage all of you to see more of them. Ring me for a list.*

Barnaby realised he had reached rock bottom when he found himself actually enjoying the entire series of *The Giant Snail Families of Antareas*. All nine episodes followed the path of a family of snails as they travelled a mile across a rocky ledge during the long Antareas winter. The more memorable episodes were 'Herman Bruises an Antenna', and the grand finale, 'Felix Reaches a Rock'. When Barnaby finished watching the last episode he found himself limping to the kitchen, wondering if he might have been happier as a snail.

That's when two events changed his life forever. His mother was watching a program in the living room about a painting destroyed in a fire. Peering over her shoulder, he almost wept when he realised the work was Dobvey's *I Looked Up and Saw a Garble*, one of his most revered pieces.

'My God,' Barnaby said. 'What a terrible loss.'

Which was when the second thing happened that changed Barnaby forever. He discovered the reason for his mother's silence: she was stone-cold dead, taken suddenly by a heart attack.

Slumping onto the couch beside her, he was surprised he didn't feel particularly upset about his mother's death. Instead, his eyes focused on the television. *I Looked Up and Saw a Garble* was lost forever, but that did not mean it could not live again.

And so began Barnaby Hazleton's second life.

After his mother's funeral, he dragged out his canvases and paints that had been languishing in the cupboard and started working on his version of the painting. Day and night he studied computerised images, applying paint to canvas with an obsessive zeal to reproduce the original. Nine months later, he staggered back from the canvas with an exhausted sigh.

I Looked Up and Saw a Garble did not just look similar to the original; it was identical in every respect.

Over the next twenty years he created dozens more copies of other famous paintings, gradually tearing out most of the underground apartment's fixtures to expand his gallery of history's greatest works.

Or, at least, his versions of history's greatest works.

At the age of forty-five, Barnaby had just completed his pièce de résistance. Five years before, someone had stolen Leonardo's *Last Supper* from its location in Old Milan. In the middle of the night, an industrious thief had removed the entire wall upon which it was painted.

Now, Barnaby stood before his version of the original. The work had been taxing. This time he had pushed himself to the limit, working for days at a time without food or sleep. In the end, however, Barnaby felt he had outdone himself. The faces of the apostles were truly expressive, exhibiting various levels of shock and dismay as Jesus revealed that one would betray him.

But it was the face of Jesus where Barnaby's talent truly prevailed.

The Messiah looked positively...*otherworldly*. While Barnaby had been working on the face he had found himself almost driven by a higher power to recreate the genius of Leonardo da Vinci.

Barnaby Hazleton had never been a religious man, but now he found himself lifting his eyes towards heaven. It seemed that God himself had blessed him with a gift and shown him the way.

'Thank you,' he said quietly.

And that's when the painting spoke to him.

What the—

Barnaby's eyes darted left and right. The basement apartment was fifty feet below ground. He had never heard a sound from beyond the walls. *Was it a voice?*

The sound came again, and Barnaby's eyes darted upwards. It seemed to come from the painting.

He approached the masterpiece on shaking legs and stared into the face of Jesus.

'Are you trying to give me a sign?' he asked.

He waited. Jesus peered down at him with a beatific expression. Barnaby had always believed in a connection between art and the divine. Was it possible that link was about to be confirmed?

Another noise came from the painting. There was no doubt about it. It *was* a voice, as if God were communicating from a great distance.

Barnaby stepped closer.

'Are you trying to tell me something? Speak to me,' Barnaby said. 'Tell me what I must do.'

The face of Jesus exploded into a thousand pieces as a large golden head smashed through the wall.

'Run!' the metal head screamed. 'Get back! It's alive!'

Barnaby staggered back from the destruction in speechless horror as the metal creature broke through the wall and leapt into the room. Barnaby turned back to the painting. It was damaged, but at least the remainder—

The entire wall toppled forward, crashing onto the floor.

Wa-woomph!

Two more people—a man and a woman—scrambled over the rubble and raced past him towards the gallery in the next room.

'Sorry about this!' the woman yelled over her shoulder. 'But you'd better get out of here.'

'We're not kidding!' the man added. 'There's something coming after us—and it's not pretty!'

I'm hallucinating, Barnaby thought. *It's a delusion brought about by the long hours of work. I'll wake up and* The Last Supper *will be perfect—*

Then the creature appeared, convincing him that this was no delusion.

'Gaarrk!' the creature bellowed as it oozed into the room.

Barnaby tried to speak, but could only open and close his mouth like a goldfish. The three people had pulled out blasters and were now firing into the opposite wall, completely destroying Paxley's *A Black Quixo in an Inky Black Cave* and Tobor's *The Massacre of Mobius Four*, to make a hole big enough to climb through.

'Run!' the woman screamed at him.

'For the love of God,' Barnaby said, finally redis-covering the power of speech. 'What is it?'

'It's a cheese sandwich,' the robot yelled back. 'Radiation has mutated it into a sentient life form!'

As the three strangers disappeared through the gap they had just blasted in the wall, Barnaby stared in horror at the creature. Up close, he realised it *was* a cheese sandwich, although it was a million times larger than any cheese sandwich in history. It had no eyes—or face, for that matter—but a rudimentary mouth ran along the centre where the slice of Swiss cheese had once been.

Zeeb says:

By strange coincidence, Barnaby Hazleton was distantly related to Bert Jackson, the workman who was responsible for tossing the sandwich down the ventilation shaft two centuries earlier.

You don't need to file that information away anywhere. I just thought you'd find it interesting.

Staggering away from the creature, Barnaby turned back only once to see it devouring the paintings he'd spent decades creating. The creature burped, emitting a stench that smelt vaguely of dead rat, Swiss cheese and oil paint.

Giving a last, wild cry, Barnaby fled for his life.

18

'I've only got one question,' Blake said to Nicki as they trudged down the darkened tunnel. 'Can you guess what it is?'

They had left the cheese sandwich far behind after the monster had headed in a different direction apparently in search of new prey.

'Uh, no,' Nicki said airily.

'Really?'

'Nothing springs to mind.'

'Let me give you a clue,' Blake said. 'Do the words, *Yippee! Come and get us, you sprot eater*, mean anything?'

'Oh,' Nicki said. 'That.'

'Yes. *That.*'

Nicki looked rather embarrassed—or as embarrassed as a gold-skinned woman could look. 'I get nervous sometimes,' she said. 'Being a cyborg, sometimes my human biology doesn't communicate properly with my psytotronic chips, and I say...inappropriate things.'

'Inappropriate...' Blake's face twitched. 'That's not inappropriate. That's come-and-hack-me-to-death-with-a-teaspoon-and-eat-my-brains-out *insane*!'

Much to his surprise, it wasn't Nicki who retaliated but Astrid. 'You can't talk,' she snapped. 'You've put your foot in it once or twice.'

'Put my foot...' Blake was incredulous. 'I've never challenged a rampaging cheese sandwich to a duel to the death!'

'You forgot about your own daughter's birthday party!'

'Will you ever forgive me for that?'

'*I* have,' she said. 'But Lisa hasn't.'

Nicki spoke up. 'I'm sorry about the *Come and get us* comment. I'm not perfect, despite my superior mental capability.'

'Saying *superior mental capability* is another example of saying inappropriate things,' Blake said.

'That's just the truth,' Nicki said. 'I am a genius a thousand times over—'

'A toaster on legs can hardly count—'

'Hey!' Astrid snapped. 'Enough is enough!'

They walked on in silence. After a while, Blake pulled out his food pills and offered them around. Astrid's eyes narrowed.

'Haggis and mushrooms?' she said. 'You've got to be kidding.'

'It's an acquired taste.'

Nicki and Astrid selected bacon and eggs.

When they reached a junction, Nicki directed them along a narrow passage, which they followed until they arrived at a wall.

'We go through here,' Nicki said.

'Are you sure?' Blake asked.

'Absolutely. There's a cave, and beyond that, GADO.'

'Okay,' Blake said, taking a deep breath. 'Let's do this.'

He raised his blaster, set it to slow burn, and aimed it at the wall. After a few seconds the wall glowed red, giving off a smell like burnt plastic, and disappeared. Gloomy light poured from the hole.

'What the—' Blake began. 'I thought there was supposed to be a cave on the other side.'

'And what is that smell?' Astrid asked, covering her nose.

Nicki inhaled. 'It appears to be a potent combination of food waste, metal fragments, shredded timber, fabric—'

'Rubbish,' Blake said.

'No, it's the truth.'

'I mean it's rubbish,' Blake said, peering through the gap. 'There are piles of it. This cave is some old underground waste dump.'

'Is there another way around?' Astrid asked.

'There is, but it would take some time,' Nicki said.

'How long?'

'Six years, eight months, four days and—'

'Looks like we're going through,' Blake said.

Once they'd climbed through the gap, Blake, Nicki and Astrid found themselves in an enormous cavern. Mounds of rubbish stretched as far as the eye could see. Huge floodlights hung from the ceiling.

Blake felt his nostrils twitching. It was the worst stench he had ever smelt.

Zeeb says:

Of course, there are worse smells, as you'd know if you'd seen my documentary Places Where You Should Not Stick Your Nose.

The smelliest place in the known universe is Graphida Nine, and it reeks so badly it has only been visited once. A spaceship from Wortaser One landed a team of astronauts there in the hopes of colonising the planet, but after disembarking, three astronauts ate their own noses, two ate each other's noses, and the remaining astronaut swallowed his own fist to escape the stench.

It really is a very smelly place.

But the smelliest thing in the universe is actually the uncovered feet of a man by the name of Alf Price who lives in Seldom-on-Tyme. He has been declared a public health hazard on no less than sixteen occasions. Anyone approaching his home must wear biohazard suits and carry their own oxygen.

Once, a mailman, new to the area, unwittingly tried to deliver letters to the premises—and his brain imploded.

In an attempt to discover the source of Alf's rancid stench, a doctor examining his feet found no less than six infectious diseases including bubonic plague, cholera and typhoid. A new species of fungus was discovered growing between his toes. When removed for examination, the sample instantly burnt through the examination jar, melted through to the centre of the planet and created a massive volcanic eruption in China, killing half a million people.

Alf takes the whole situation in his stride. 'My feet don't bother me,' he explains. 'I just suck the grunge off when they get real bad.'

An enormous multi-coloured hill lay to their left.

'Is that what I think it is?' Blake asked.

'Only if you think it's an enormous pile of socks,' Nicki said.

'An enormous pile of *odd* socks.' Astrid pointed. 'Could this be where all the odd socks go?'

Zeeb says:

The answer is: yes and no. Every sock is part of a pair, which really does make you wonder where the other sock ends up. This remained a mystery until a scientist on the planet Varoom conducted an experiment in which he kept a pair of socks under twenty-seven-hour-a-day surveillance until one of them mysteriously vanished.

Further investigation revealed that odd socks were being sucked through an inter-dimensional porthole to the other side of the galaxy. It seems this had been going on for a long time. Thousands of years. So what do you get when you stick millions of socks together in space?

A sock planet.

And that's actually what it's called. Sock World. Which is hardly surprising, really. I mean, what else would you call it? It wouldn't be called Bulbulous Seven or Quanda Four, would it?

They slowly rounded the hill. It was only one of many similar piles spread around the cavern, all neatly catalogued into their respective types: furniture, cars, mobile phones, shoes.

Nicki stopped and frowned at her datapad. 'Oh dear,' she said. 'We're getting some weird magnetic interference.'

'Which means?' Astrid asked.

'We're lost.'

'*Sprot*,' Blake said. They were miles underground and time was running out.

'Wait!' Nicki said. 'I just saw something move!'

She pointed at a mountain of toilet bowls. Blake pulled out his blaster, but everything was still.

'Are you sure?' he asked.

A noise came from behind. Turning, Blake saw a skinny man in a pinstripe suit. His stun weapon was aimed at the three of them.

Then everything went white.

When Blake woke up, he found himself lying on a hospital gurney, his hands secured at his sides by handcuffs. It felt like he'd been asleep for hours, even the whole night. He spotted Astrid on the bed opposite, unconscious. Nicki lay on the floor, looking like a Barbie doll, her eyes open but unseeing.

They were in a room carved out of a pile of television sets, robot parts, kitchen appliances and washing machines. Between two ancient robot torsos was a mechanical rat peering down at them. It gave Blake a startled look and scurried away.

What the sprot is going on?

The little man who had shot them entered the room. He was unusually gaunt, with thinning black hair and bushy eyebrows. Beneath those eyebrows were staring eyes that reminded Blake of a fish.

'You've awoken,' the man said. 'I'm so pleased.'

'I'm Blake Carter, an officer with the PBI, and I'm placing you under—'

'Your upworld business does not concern me,' the man interrupted in a high voice. 'I am Doctor Robert Roberts and you are my guest.'

'Is that a stutter?'

Roberts shook his head. 'Merely an unfortunate name.'

'I demand that you release us immediately!' Blake said, trying to keep calm. His eyes shifted to Astrid. 'If you've harmed one hair on her head—'

'Please don't be concerned,' Roberts said, looking pained. 'I assure you I have no intention of causing you harm.'

'I'm glad.'

'But I am going to eat you.'

'Well, that's... What did you say?'

'I'm going to eat you,' Robert Roberts said, smiling as if they were discussing the weather. *It's been rather cold today...might be a change later...must bring the washing in off the line...* 'I don't know why I do it,' Roberts continued. 'Plenty of food comes down the waste disposal chutes, but I've developed rather a liking for human flesh.'

'Oh.'

'Your death will be painless.'

'Great.'

'But the cooking process will be agony. I mean, slow frying is probably the most painful way to die.

With any luck, you'll pass out after about an hour, but some have regained consciousness at inappropriate moments.'

'Well, we wouldn't want that…'

'I do need to ask you something,' Roberts said, suddenly concerned. 'Are you allergic to anything?'

'Why do you ask?'

'Well, I usually like to sprinkle on a little oregano and paprika. I'd hate to put you through any discomfort.'

'I do have an allergy,' Blake said. 'Death!'

'Oh, how droll,' Roberts gave a wheezy laugh. 'I love a meal with a sense of humour. I'll leave you now and return when the oven's ready.'

'You do that.'

Once Roberts had gone, Blake fell back onto the bed and struggled against the restraints.

Astrid's eyes fluttered open. 'Blake?' she groaned. 'What happened?'

'We got attacked by a loony with a stun gun.'

'That explains my head. I feel like I've been run over by a herd of quantors.'

Zeeb says:

> *My aunt Lily was run over by a herd of quantors. Take my word for it. It's very unpleasant.*

'How do we get out of here?' Astrid asked. 'And what's that smell?'

A strange odour drifted down the tunnel. Blake suspected the doctor was building up a fire in the cooker where he had disposed of his previous victims.

'Oh, that,' Blake said, swallowing. 'He's probably getting dinner ready.'

'Great. I'm starving. What're we having?'

'If I tell you, do you promise to remain calm?'

'Sure.'

Blake told her and Astrid fainted.

19

A plan was forming in Blake's mind, but he needed Astrid to help him carry it out. Unfortunately that would be difficult because she was still unconscious.

'Astrid! Wake up!'

She groaned and peered at him through half-open eyes. 'Please tell me this is a terrible dream.'

'This is a terrible dream.'

'Really?'

'No. We're trapped in a cave and about to be eaten by a cannibal!'

'And to think I was worried about my hair.'

'I've got a plan,' Blake said, nodding towards Nicki. 'I think she's only stunned. With any luck, she'll have a reset button. Maybe you can reach it.'

'What do you think I'm made of? Rubber?'

'Reach out with your foot! Kicking someone when they're down should be easy for you!'

Grumbling under her breath, Astrid angled her body off the gurney, stretching out so her foot almost reached Nicki. 'Where's this reset button, then?'

'Probably behind her neck.'

A sound came from the entrance to the cavern.

'He's coming back,' Blake hissed.

A moment later the doctor returned to find Astrid still unconscious on the bed, while Blake whistled innocently at the ceiling.

The doctor eyed him with suspicion. 'You're looking very pleased with yourself.'

'Just thinking about being eaten.'

'And?'

Blake lowered his voice. 'May I make a confession?'

'Yes.'

'I've had a secret desire ever since I was a boy,' Blake said. 'It might sound odd, but I've always wanted to be the victim of a cannibal.'

Robert Roberts did a double take. 'Really?'

'It's hard to explain, but it has always held a fascination for me,' Blake said. 'You won't anaesthetise me first, will you?'

'Not at all. I like my food live.'

'Good,' Blake said, feigning relief. 'So when can you start?'

'Right now, if you like.'

'Wonderful!'

'But the woman will be first.'

'What?'

'I prefer the taste of female flesh,' Roberts explained. 'It's rather more tender, and I have a new port and stilton sauce I'd like to try.'

Roberts wheeled Astrid's gurney past Blake, who caught a glimpse of her horrified face.

'Time for dinner!' the doctor said cheerily as they disappeared from the room.

Blake slumped, despairing. He couldn't reach Nicki, and he soon realised the doctor had placed their backpacks and blasters in a pile near the entrance.

But Roberts didn't know about Louis.

Louis was the backup weapon Blake had strapped to his ankle. Pushing his shoes off, he used his toes to unclip the holster and pull out the Louis .457 laser pistol. In serious combat situations it was useless, but it could still punch a hole in someone at close range.

Blake grunted. The gun slipped from his grasp onto the floor. He leant over the edge of the bed and tried to grab it again between his toes.

Almost. Just a few more inches…

The gun went off and a laser beam seared his forehead.

'*Aahh! Sprotting krog of a sprot's—*'

Roberts' voice echoed down the tunnel. 'Everything okay down there?'

'Oh, yes,' Blake said. 'Just filled with excitement about being eaten by a cannibal. *Weeee!*'

He tried to grab the weapon again. *I'll be lucky if I don't take off my head*, he thought.

Just down the corridor, Astrid was also struggling as Robert Roberts attached her gurney to a conveyor belt that led to a fiery oven.

'The gas is provided free of charge via the methane produced by the rubbish,' Roberts said. He gave her leg a pinch. 'So tender! Just how I like it!'

Astrid tried to think of a way to stall him, but she could only wonder how she had ended up here. The day had started so normally. A few hours teaching, a spot of shopping, a touch-up by her nail technician—and now she was trapped in an underground lair about to be eaten by a cannibal.

A pile of bones lay in a corner. She didn't want to imagine where they'd come from. She had to delay Roberts long enough for Blake to save her—if he could.

'So have you seen anything good on television?' she asked shrilly.

The doctor paused. 'There are a few shows I rather like.'

'Really?' Astrid stared into the burning oven. 'What are they?'

'Oh...' He paused a moment, thinking. 'There's that reality-TV show on Channel 979 about the interspecies family living on Eradranabran. Traskian on the father's side—'

'—and Zybrat on the mother's!'

'You've seen it?'

'Absolutely! It's wonderful, all those little half-mammal, half-lizard children.'

'And there's so many of them!'

'I know,' she said. 'Is it sixteen or seventeen?'

'It was seventeen, but one of them broke a leg—'

'I remember!' Astrid said. 'And they ate him on the spot!'

She stopped. It had seemed so amusing on a reality-TV program set on a world thousands of light years away, but now it was rather too close to home.

'And what else do you like?' she asked.

'Oh, the cooking shows.'

Astrid tried to speak, but all she could see was the lizard kid disappearing under a pile of hungry siblings.

The doctor gave a satisfied sigh, pushed a button and the conveyor began to move.

This can't be happening!

'Please! Think about what you're doing!'

'I am,' Roberts said. 'It's making me hungry!'

'No, no, it's wrong! Taking a human life is wrong!'

'Not if you do it out of necessity.'

'You're doing it out of necessity?'

'Absolutely. Pizza Hut won't deliver down here.'

The conveyor belt inched along, dragging her closer to the oven.

No! It can't end like this!

'Please!' she begged. 'You have to listen to me! It's wrong to kill. It's wrong to eat people. Every life is important. Everyone counts.'

She found herself staring directly into the eyes of Robert Roberts. Slowly, he reached over and pushed a button. The conveyor belt slid to a halt with Astrid only inches away from the flames.

'You've made me realise—' the doctor said.

'Thank God!'

'—that I haven't added my oregano or my paprika! How could I forget? And a pinch of salt makes all the difference!'

He reached for a jar, but his carefully laid plans were soon derailed when a laser beam winged him. Stunned, Roberts reached into his pocket and withdrew a device the size of a remote control just as Blake and Nicki burst from a tunnel. Roberts pressed a button on the device and disappeared into thin air.

'Astrid!' Blake yelled.

Nicki released her and Astrid threw herself into Blake's arms. Drawing back, she stared at his forehead.

'What happened to you?' she asked.

'I was able to get out my other weapon. I had some problems firing it, though. Grazed myself. Then I shot Nicki.'

'You shot Nicki!'

'He's wanted to do it from the moment we met,' Nicki said.

143

'There's probably some truth in that,' Blake admitted. 'But I did do it on purpose. Knowing she'd only been stunned by Roberts, I remembered—'

'—that robots have automatic defence systems,' Nicki said. 'While I'm not a robot, the part of me that is has the same software. I woke up, released Blake and we came to your rescue.'

'So what happened to the doctor?' Astrid asked. 'He disappeared into thin air.'

'I have no idea,' Blake said. 'Maybe we'll never know.'

Zeeb says:

> *Allow me to fill you in on the details.*
>
> *Robert Roberts owned a site-to-site teleportation device, designed to transport him to the far side of the underground cavern. In a bizarre twist of fate, however, a hole in the fabric of space-time intersected with the matter transportation beam, carrying him away to a planet in the southern arm of the Pegasus galaxy, where he landed in the middle of a reality-TV show called* Lizard Survivor. *He lived there for three days, pursued by gangs of three-foot-high reptiles.*
>
> *Finally, cornered in a desolate canyon, he was torn to pieces and eaten alive.*
>
> *His final words, 'Don't forget the oregano!' were broadcast to the ten-billion-strong audience, and even made it onto the* Best of Lizard Survivor, *despite the audience having no clue as to their meaning.*

'Where to from here?' Blake asked.

'I saw a jamming device in Roberts' cave,' Nicki said. 'I think that's what caused that magnetic interference. I'll turn it off.'

Nicki left. Blake stared at Astrid. Her hair was dishevelled, her nails broken; she had dirt on her face and her clothing was ruined.

He thought she'd never looked lovelier.

She frowned. 'Don't look at me like that.'

'Like what?'

'You know,' she said, her voice low. 'With mushy eyes.'

'I can't help it. You're beautiful.'

'I look like a mess!'

'When all this is over, maybe we should think about—'

Nicki reappeared. 'The jamming device is off!'

Blake sighed. His timing was never good.

'So where are we, then?' he asked Nicki. 'And how do we get out of here?'

'I'm not completely sure,' she said, scanning her datapad. 'Roberts must have a second jamming device, but it looks like there's a wall about a mile east of here. We can cut through there and hopefully get our bearings.'

Once they'd retrieved their backpacks, the trio set off again through the piles of junk and reached the wall soon after. Nicki fired her weapon, creating a hole that revealed another dark corridor beyond.

'I can see where we are now,' Nicki said, checking

her map. 'We don't need to take this tunnel. There's a small cave on the other side of this wall. We'll save time by cutting across.'

She fired her weapon again, this time dissolving the wall. But instead of darkness, bright sunshine poured through the gap and a gentle breeze washed against their faces.

'What the—' Astrid started.

'This doesn't make any sense,' Nicki said.

'That wouldn't be the first time today,' Blake muttered.

20

Beyond the gap lay a broad, green valley with a stream running through it. Trees laden with honey-coloured flowers and wide patches of shamrock green lawn carpeted the hills. The sky was arctic blue, laced with milky-white clouds. A flock of red-and-yellow birds swooped between the trees and disappeared into the distance.

'This we don't need,' Blake said.

'What the sprot is it?' Astrid asked, amazed. 'Where are we? Are we still underground?'

'Yes and no,' Nicki said. 'I think it's a pocket dimension.'

Blake checked his watch. He had less than a day until Badde's deadline expired. They couldn't afford a detour, especially a pocket dimension leading to another world.

Zeeb says:

Coincidentally, 'A Pocket Dimension Leading to Another World' was a number one hit by the group Hoby Toblat and the Bargs. It stayed at the top of the charts for three months before being usurped by the Vienna Boys' Choir version of the Village People hit 'In the Navy'.

'Isn't there a way around this?' Blake asked Nicki.

'Not unless you brought a strontium drill with you.'

Blake frowned. A detour through a pocket dimension had not been on the cards, but this wasn't the first time he'd come across one.

'These things have multiple exits,' he said. 'We can always come back here if we don't find one.'

Astrid and Nicki climbed through the hole. 'Are you coming?' Nicki asked Blake.

Blake stepped onto a green meadow. The portal they'd just travelled through was sunk into a boulder at the top of a hill.

It was midday, wherever they were, and it wasn't Earth. No place on Earth had looked this way for centuries. He looked up to see three moons in the sky.

Definitely not Earth.

'Hey!' Astrid cried.

The hole was now shrinking.

'No!' Blake yelled.

Before he could take another step the hole had shrunk to nothing, giving a tiny *puck* as it slipped out of existence. Blake punched the boulder.

'I've never seen that happen before,' he said.

Nicki stroked her chin. 'It's estimated that holes leading into pocket dimensions close once every 2183 times,' she said. 'Looks like this is one of those times.'

'What are we going to do?' Astrid asked.

'I'm not sure,' Blake said.

'You said there'd be a way out!'

'I'm sure there is, but we've got to find it!'

'Excuse me,' Nicki said.

'What if we don't?' Astrid asked.

'We will,' Blake said.

'But if we don't—'

Nicki intervened. 'We may have a problem.'

To Blake's way of thinking, being stuck on an alien world in an unknown part of the galaxy with no means of escape and only twelve hours to break into the most secure facility on Earth was *already* a problem.

'A person just came out of that house,' Nicki said, pointing. 'And he has a weapon.'

Blake had not noticed the house, nestled between trees halfway down the hill. From this distance it looked like some kind of ancient log cabin.

'You're right,' Blake said. 'He *does* have a weapon. An axe, I think.'

'This'll sound strange,' Astrid said. 'But he looks... familiar.'

On the other side of the field, the man who had just stepped from his woodshed to chop some logs peered up to see something unusual. Three people were standing in the middle of his field. One of them was a golden robot. The other two were humans—a man and a woman.

It had been a long time since the man had seen anyone different, and this made him feel a little scared, but also hopeful. He started up the field.

'He's coming this way,' Nicki said.

'I can see that,' Blake said.

'Maybe we should shoot him.'

'*Whaaat?*'

'A study conducted last year by the First Contacts Public Review Board found that violence was the outcome of some eighty-two per cent of first-contact situations. Its main recommendation was to shoot first.'

'And ask questions later?' Astrid said. 'Keep your blaster holstered, cowgirl.'

'I agree,' Blake said. 'No shooting unless we have to.'

'What if he does something threatening?' Nicki asked.

'Like what?'

'Oh, you know. Looks at us funny.'

'*Looks at us funny?*'

'You know, funny I-want-to-chop-you-up funny.'

Blake sighed. 'Don't do anything.'

The man continued towards them. The occasional word was carried by the breeze to him, words like *shoot* and *funny*, and then he heard the word *cannibal*. But he was not unduly concerned. He had lived a long time—long past his time, truth be told—and he didn't fear death.

He stopped about ten feet away. Their surprise was understandable. He was probably the last person they ever expected to see.

'Howdy, there,' he said. 'I'm Elvis Presley. Welcome to Elvisworld.'

21

'It was a dark and stormy night,' Elvis began.

They were sitting on the deck of the cottage on the other side of the hill. From here they had a clear view of a narrow valley. A few purple cows stood in the field, thoughtfully chewing grass. Something that looked like a red parrot with four legs coasted on the wind overhead and landed on a tree.

Elvis had made them sandwiches, which they'd devoured. Now he poured them drinks of cold lemonade from a jug.

'I was at Gracelands making a deep-fried peanut-butter sandwich,' he said. 'It was late and everyone else had gone to bed. I was feeling poorly, which was not unusual back in those days.' He slapped his trim belly. 'I went through a bit of a bad patch, you might say.'

Elvis went on to explain that he had been about to head upstairs to catch some shut-eye when he'd heard an odd sound behind him. He'd turned to see a small black hole appear in the air on the far side of his kitchen. Within seconds it had taken up half the room, and then a man in a laboratory coat had stepped out, clapping his hands in delight.

'Hello, 1977. Goodbye, 2082.'

Elvis had been so surprised he dropped his deep-fried peanut-butter sandwich. 'Who in tarnation are you?' he asked.

'I'm Professor John Galwick and I'm here to save you.'

'From what?'

'From yourself.'

Galwick explained that he had come from the future in a time machine of his own invention to save the king of rock 'n' roll because he didn't have long to live.

When Elvis asked, he wouldn't say how long.

Zeeb says:

   Time travel is, of course, illegal. There are serious punishments, depending on what part of the galaxy you happen to reside in. For example, anyone found tampering with the laws of time on Elidor Minor is punished by a thousand years in the Toovian sludge pits before being drawn and quartered.

Of course, punishments don't stop people from breaking the law. Many individuals have tried to tamper with time over the years, but it always ends in disaster.

On Earth, so many people have tried to save John F. Kennedy from being assassinated that at one point the former president was found to be both travelling in the motorcade in Dallas and shooting at himself from the nearby grassy knoll.

Likewise, multitudes have tried to kill Hitler. In one parallel timeline the Führer ended up becoming a female singer and performing 'We'll Meet Again' before Winston Churchill at 10 Downing Street in the middle of World War II.

You can see why it's best to leave things as they are.

'I can offer you salvation,' Professor Galwick had explained to Elvis.

'You mean like Jesus?'

'Better than Jesus.'

'No one's better than Jesus,' Elvis said. 'Except, maybe, Little Richard.'

The plan was simple—or, at least, simple to someone travelling backwards in time from the year 2082. Galwick wanted to scan Elvis's body and take a DNA sample. After returning to his own time, he would introduce Elvis to a whole new generation.

As Elvis saw it, he didn't have too many choices—

especially if he was about to become a lead singer with the band upstairs.

So John Galwick scanned Elvis with his Hyper-Tensile DNA Reader. After taking the sample, Galwick produced a copy using a portable matter creation synthesiser, and Elvis soon found himself staring at his naked doppelgänger.

'I've never looked better,' Elvis said.

The Hyper-Tensile DNA Reader had recreated his body just as it would have been without all the deep-fried peanut-butter sandwiches and prescription drugs.

'I *feel* better,' Elvis Two had said, staring in amazement at himself. 'Like I could live forever.'

'And you will,' Galwick said.

'Sounds like a good deal all round,' the real Elvis said, rubbing his stomach. He let out an unruly burp. 'Pardon me, folks. I might go upstairs. I'm feeling a mite poorly.'

'A trip to the bathroom might be in order,' Galwick gently suggested.

'I might just do that.'

'Then we'll be on our way.'

They said their goodbyes, and Galwick and the clone skipped back to the 21st century while Elvis hobbled up to the bathroom to claim his throne for the final time.

The rest is history. Or should have been.

'I remember reading about the Elvis craze in the history books,' Blake said, stroking his chin thoughtfully. 'There were said to be upwards of a million Elvises on Earth.'

'There were more,' Elvis said. 'Many more. Eventually, we were herded up like *hound dogs* and brought here.' He paused. 'That's a little Elvis humour for you.'

'Yeah, that's great. Where is here, exactly?'

'We call it Elvisworld,' Elvis said. 'But it's actually an inter-dimensional pocket in time and space.'

'We need to get back home,' Astrid told him, and explained about Lisa's kidnapping and their need to break into GADO.

'I'd love to help you people,' Elvis said, 'but I don't know how. If we could leave here, we would.'

'Actually, I've been working on this,' Nicki said. 'I think there *is* a way out.'

'We'll do everything we can,' Elvis said, giving Astrid a small smile. 'Though I gotta admit, little lady, I'm kinda *stuck on you*.' He paused again. 'That's Elvis humour, with a touch of flirting.'

'Why, thank you, Mr Elvis.'

'Just call me Elvis. All my friends do.'

'Talking about your friends,' Blake interrupted. 'How many of you are there?'

'I'm not rightly sure,' Elvis said. 'All the different types are here.'

'The *different types*?' Astrid repeated.

'There have been lots of mutations since we arrived,' Elvis said vaguely. He turned to Nicki. 'Do you think we could leave too?'

'If we can, you can,' Nicki said. 'But aren't you happy here?'

'We're not unhappy. But we'd love to see what Earth is like now. Especially if it's part of some intergalactic club. It's fair to say we'd like to *return to sender*.'

Elvis winked.

Leaving the valley, they followed a trail towards a town on the coast. Here people worked in the fields, planting crops and harvesting grain. They were all different kinds of Elvises. Fat Elvis, thin Elvis, tall and short Elvis, male and—

'What the sprot?' Blake exclaimed.

A woman gave them a wave from a doorway.

'Like I said,' Elvis said. 'Mutations.'

There were people who looked a lot like Elvis—and plenty who only slightly resembled the King. Blake began to think of their Elvis as Woodsman Elvis.

Fifteen minutes later, they reached a town. 'We're going to see the King of Kings,' Woodsman Elvis explained.

'God?' Nicki asked. 'Good. There's some stuff I want to complain about. Hunger, pestilence, drought—'

'No, no. The king of Elvisworld.'

'So where do we find him?' Blake asked.

'Just down the end here.' Elvis motioned to a sign that read *Lonely Street*. 'At the *Heartbreak Hotel*.'

Another wink.

Blake sidled up to Nicki. 'I'm not sure how much more of this I can take,' he murmured.

'What's wrong with you, Blake?' Nicki asked. 'What

157

have you got? A *wooden heart*? Get it? *Wooden heart*?'

'I'm in hell,' Blake groaned. 'Elvis hell.'

At the hotel, another Elvis clone led them to a penthouse overlooking the coastline. The ocean was sparkling blue. A school of animals that looked like dolphins—only with six fins—frolicked in the water. Seagulls as big as albatross dived for fish in the ocean.

Elvisworld was one of the more genial places Blake had seen. The world had been selected to imprison the Elvis population, but not to kill them off.

Still, Blake thought. *Marooning these people here for all eternity is cruel no matter how you swing it.*

The king of Elvisworld sported a handlebar moustache. 'Howdy, folks,' he said. 'It's nice to see a new face for a change.'

Blake explained their dilemma.

'So what can we do?' the king asked.

'I have a plan,' Nicki said. 'I've identified an exit portal off the coast. We can use it to return to Earth.'

'I've never seen any sort of portal,' the king said.

'It can only be opened under the right circumstances,' Nicki told him. 'A sonic resonance blast would force it open long enough for us to jump through and return.'

'How do we make this blast?' Woodsman Elvis asked.

Nicki explained.

'You've got to be kidding,' Blake groaned.

Later that afternoon, they all assembled on a cliff overlooking the coast. A stiff wind blew sea spray onto

Blake's face as he peered over the edge. Hundreds of feet below he spotted a rocky platform.

Blake swallowed. *If this plan doesn't work, there'll be no second chances.*

Speaking of second chances, his gaze crossed to Astrid. Woodsman Elvis seemed to have taken a real liking to her. Blake drew her aside.

'How're you coping?' he asked.

'Fine.' They had been married long enough for her to know when something was up. She peered at Blake suspiciously. 'What do you mean?'

'Elvis seems to have taken a shine to you.'

'He has a certain attraction to me,' she admitted. 'He describes it as a kind of *burning love.*'

She stifled a laugh.

'Astrid,' Blake said. 'Think of what you're doing. You can't just go batting your pretty eyes at every Elvis that comes along.'

'Jealous?'

He didn't reply. He *was* jealous. Old feelings died hard and it wasn't easy seeing his ex-wife being wooed by one of history's greatest performers.

'Just don't start anything you can't finish.'

'I won't,' she promised. 'But you know how it is. Sometimes you just *can't help falling in love.*'

'Dear God...' Blake peered up at the sky. 'Take me now. Please.'

*

Over the next hour, thousands of Elvises gathered at the headland. The king had sent the word out and the people had answered. Blake hoped Nicki's plan was not just a figment of her mechanised imagination.

'Are you sure this is going to work?' he asked her.

'We've got a seventy-thirty chance.'

'A seventy per cent chance of survival?'

'Um...'

'Forget I asked.'

Woodsman Elvis gave Astrid a kiss on the cheek. As he gently released her hand, he gave Blake a guilty look. 'Just saying goodbye to a beautiful woman,' he explained.

'That's fine,' Blake said. He didn't have anything against Elvis. He'd gone out of his way to help them, and Blake wanted the best for him. 'I want to thank you for everything.'

'You're welcome, partner,' Woodsman Elvis said. 'And you've shown us a way out too.' They shook hands. 'Thank you—thank you very much.'

The king quietened the crowd as Nicki climbed onto a high rock to speak. The numbers had swelled in the last few minutes and there were now tens of thousands of Elvises spread all the way into town and onto the beach. Blake felt unnerved seeing so many versions of the same face.

'We are going to need a High C!' Nicki yelled to those who could hear her. 'And you need to sustain it for as long as possible!'

The instruction spread through the crowd like a wave.

Nicki climbed down from the rock and the king took her place.

'We're going to send our guests off in style,' he said, raising an arm. 'You heard the lady. High C for as long as we can hold it. On a count of three. One...two...'

He dropped his arm.

'Three!'

'*Ahhhhhhhhh!*'

The wall of sound struck Blake. He peered over the edge of the cliff. Nothing was happening. Nicki signalled to the king to increase the volume—and within seconds the sound grew deafening.

Gripping Blake's arm, Nicki pointed at a spot fifty feet below where a swirling mist had begun to form. A black line appeared in the middle.

'It's working!' Blake shouted. He nodded encouragement to the king and the sound grew even louder.

The hole widened. Grabbing Astrid and Nicki, Blake led them to the edge. If they missed the hole, they would plummet to their deaths. Blake swallowed the lump in his throat.

How do I get into these situations?

Taking a deep breath, he prepared to jump. Then, remembering some unfinished business, he turned back to Woodsman Elvis.

'*It's now or never!*' Blake cried. 'Get it? *It's now or never!*'

They jumped.

22

'Here's your chicken,' Badde said peevishly. 'The Game Prism's on order. It won't arrive till Friday.'

Lisa sighed. 'I suppose that'll have to do.'

A whole day had passed and Lisa was starving. She had even begun to wonder if Badde had abandoned her. She ate three pieces of chicken without looking up once. Finally, chewing on a drumstick, she noticed Badde staring at her through the bars.

'Do you want some?' she offered. 'There's plenty.'

'No, thanks,' Badde said. 'I'm trying to watch my weight. Evil geniuses always have to look their best.'

'For when you get caught?'

'I won't get caught. Nobody knows my real name or what I look like.'

'Bartholomew Badde isn't your real name?'

'I'm afraid not. I needed something catchy, something that would roll off the tongue, something that would resonate with the newsreaders, and my real name wasn't it.'

Lisa took a sip of Hypergo. 'So what's happening in the outside world?'

'The usual. Delgar Five won the Interleague Baseball Pennant. The president of Rastarus has resigned due to corruption charges.'

'So nothing's changed.'

'Not really,' he agreed. 'There's one odd story, though—a fifty-foot cheese sandwich is rampaging through the lower east side of Neo City.'

'No kidding?' Lisa's eyes angled to the single window. It looked like it was getting dark out there. 'Only in Neo City.'

An agreeable silence played out between them. Badde had seemed like a badass in the beginning when he made her watch the *Brady Bunch* episodes, but now he seemed almost companionable.

'You could always let me go,' Lisa said.

'I could, but I won't. You're a very small but important cog in my plans to destroy the human race. While my actions have resulted in terrible destruction over the years, I've never actually caused the ruination of an entire planet. Can you imagine how I'll be remembered?'

'As a fruitcake?'

He ignored her. 'When I'm done, they will speak about Earth in glowing terms: of the rise of life here, the evolution of the human species, the development of civilisation, and then—*kapow*!'

'*Kapow?*'

'The end of the world.' Badde sniffed. 'Doesn't happen every day.'

Lisa frowned. 'Why do you do such awful things?'

'It's a long and involved story,' Badde said, not meeting her eye now. 'I'm just made that way.'

'That's a load of sprot! You can choose to be whoever you want!'

Oh God, Lisa thought. *I sound just like my mother!*

'You don't have to be an evil villain,' she continued. 'What if you used your superpowers for good rather than evil?'

'I don't have any superpowers.'

'You know what I mean,' Lisa said. 'What made you become a villain?'

'A terrible childhood. I was beaten and made to eat rats for dinner.'

'Really?'

'No, I just like being evil.'

Badde seemed ready to keep talking, but then he froze. For a full five seconds he stared blankly into space, as if listening to some inner voice. Finally he broke out of it and glared at her.

'I don't have to answer your questions,' he said. 'You're the hostage and I'm the, er, hostage-taker.'

'I was only trying—'

He strode to the door. 'We shouldn't become too friendly.'

'Why?'

'If your father doesn't retrieve Maria for me, I'll be forced to hurt you,' he said. 'Badly.' He paused. 'No pun intended.'

After he had left, Lisa sat in the silent cell, a cold piece of chicken in her hand.

Oh dear, she thought. *This might get really grim. He might even have episodes of* Gungler's Planet.

Zeeb says:

> *Gungler's Planet is probably the worst television show ever made. It's about a family travelling through space to start a new life on a distant planet, but they end up crashing somewhere. There is only one type of food available: small, red berries they imaginatively christen 'the red berries'.*

> *Every day is spent searching for the berries. Each and every day. Day after day. There are no monsters on the planet. There are no alien visitors or ancient civilisations or cool spaceships they can use to escape. It's simply a big, dusty planet with the occasional cluster of berries. No one dies. No one even gets sick.*

> *After a while, viewers hated the show so much they started sending letters to the network demanding the torture and death of the main characters.*

Despite all this, it was strangely addictive.
People found they could not stop themselves from
watching the program. Some people even recorded
it so they wouldn't miss an episode. In the end the
show was cancelled—not because of low ratings,
but because it was causing so many brain seizures.

That hasn't stopped its ongoing success. It's
always in syndication. Somewhere.

I've got to get out of here, Lisa thought.

Discarding the chicken, she began searching her cell for a way out. It didn't take long. The floor was concrete. Building materials had come a long way, but good old-fashioned concrete just seemed to stick around. Using her fingernails, she could probably scratch a tunnel through in about a century.

The ceiling looked the same, but she shinnied up the bars and checked the roof anyway. *Sprot!* She tried shaking the bars. They didn't budge. Unless she grew metal teeth, there was no way to get through.

This left only the back wall.

Lisa tapped the wall. Surprisingly, it sounded hollow. She glanced back towards the door. Hiding an enormous hole wouldn't be easy. Shame she didn't have a painting to hang over it. If only there was a way for it not to be seen...

Peering under the bed, she realised there was enough room for her to slide under. Each time Badde had come to her cell, she had heard his footsteps echoing down the corridor. It took the best part of thirty seconds. That would be long enough to jump back onto the bed and start filing her nails or humming a happy tune.

Badde had given her a knife and fork for the chicken. For an evil genius, he wasn't very bright. She retrieved these and started to scrape at the wall with the knife. Like most things these days, the wall was made from plastic. It only took a minute to make a coin-sized hole. Half an hour later, it was the size of her head.

But it was starting to get dark. *Sprot.* She needed light. Badde had taken her wristcomm, but at least she still had her hairclip. It had a built-in light and a music player.

She flicked a switch, and it started to flash blue and white. *Great.* She poked the hairclip through the gap and saw another barrier made of the same plastic.

Here goes…

She dug at the second wall with the knife. After several minutes, she managed to poke her fist through.

Yes!

Cold air flowed across her fingers.

A sound came from behind. *Footsteps!*

Scrambling out from under the bed, Lisa threw herself onto the mattress and started humming.

Badde came to the door, carrying a bag.

'Everything okay?' he asked.

'Fine,' she said, frowning. 'Why?'

'No reason.' He eyed her suspiciously. 'What's that in your hand?'

'Oh, this?' She was still holding the hairclip. At least the light was off. 'Just a little thing I use to keep my hair under control.' She gathered her hair up into a bun. 'What do you think looks best? Up? Or down?'

'I have absolutely no idea,' Badde hissed. 'I'm an evil genius, not a hairdresser! Anyway, I just wanted to drop something off.'

He passed the bag through the bars.

'More Hypergo!' Lisa said. 'Thanks.'

'Enjoy it while you can,' Badde said. 'Time's running out.'

23

Blake Carter was confused.

After falling through the inter-dimensional gap in Elvisworld, he'd expected simply to leap back into the general vicinity of GADO. Instead he found himself falling down an endless black tunnel—and was now somehow looking at the back of his own head.

I'm getting a bald spot, he thought. *I should do something about that.*

Blinking, he realised he was looking at a version of himself who was looking at the back of another Blake Carter who was, in turn, looking at the one before him... His fall was being repeated ad infinitum.

It was very strange.

'What's going on?' infinite numbers of himself asked.

Suddenly Nicki's disembodied head floated past. 'It looks like there's an irregularity of the inter-dimensional rift,' she explained. 'Like a piece of food stuck in your throat.'

'This is odd.' Astrid's voice seemed to come from nowhere.

Blake looked down and realised that Astrid was floating through his torso.

'What the hell are you doing?' he demanded.

'I can't help it. And since when did you start wearing boxer shorts?'

'Mind your own business.'

He hoped his underwear was clean. Looking down the tunnel, he saw a pinpoint of light, growing larger every second. At its centre was a man sitting at a very untidy desk. Trays of paper on both sides of the desk were overflowing. He had a map of the Earth pinned to the wall behind him.

The man looked like a dishevelled poodle. His white hair and beard lurched in all directions as if it hadn't seen a comb in twenty years. On the desk before him were piles of paper two feet high. This man, completely unaware of what was heading towards him, was in fact Colonel Walter Lichenstein. He was in charge of the western security division of GADO.

Some at GADO said that the colonel was past it, but they never said it loudly. Those who voiced such opinions usually found themselves guarding ice in Siberia or manning a station on Pluto, courtesy of Walter's brother-in-law, Sam Feldspar, GADO's director.

Those who knew Walter well sometimes tactfully suggested to him that he might be happier playing golf at the Silver Links course on Risa Three, or holidaying with a blue-rinsed companion on the beaches of Palamarus.

He was, after all, 107 years old.

Walter Lichenstein ignored such advice. That would have been a dereliction of duty, and Walter was nothing if not a dedicated soldier. He could trace his heritage back to the time of Nelson. A cousin, many times removed, had fought and died bravely at the Battle of Trafalgar.

Zeeb says:

Fought and died bravely? Not exactly. History records him as attempting to desert as HMS Victory sailed into battle. Stepping into a lifeboat, he slipped, hit his head, fell into the water and drowned.

As far as Lichenstein was concerned, good soldiers did not leave their post. He turned up for work every day at 8am without fail, drank a cup of Siberian tea, ate a piece of reconstituted bread (no butter) and proceeded to issue orders for the day to the multitude of subordinates operating in his section.

He would have been most surprised to learn that few of those orders were ever followed. 'Shoot everyone with blue eyes' or 'Hand me a pair of boxer shorts—I'm feeling hungry' or 'Let's declare war on Germany! I don't like their sausages!' were, wisely, ignored.

His life in the military had taken him to strange places where he had seen strange things and done strange things. So he was not too worried when, peering over a pile of paperwork, he saw three people flying down an inter-dimensional tunnel towards him.

They crashed into his desk, sent papers flying and knocked over a filing cabinet.

'New recruits, eh what?' Colonel Lichenstein snapped.

'Pardon?' Blake said, as they scrambled to their feet.

'New recruits? First day on the job, eh?'

'Yes,' Blake said, looking sideways at Nicki and Astrid. 'Absolutely.'

'Names!'

'Smith,' Blake said.

'Uh,' Astrid said.

'Rumpelstiltskin,' Nicki said.

'Smith, Uh and Rumpelstiltskin,' the colonel said. 'You're the sorriest trio of recruits I've ever seen.'

'Yes,' Blake agreed.

'That's *Yes, sir!*'

'Yes, sir!' the three responded.

Blake could not believe his luck.

Zeeb says:

> *Luck is a funny thing. So is coincidence. On the planet Elligor Minor, an eerily similar set of*

*circumstances was also occurring. Three people
from Telangor Seven had fallen through an inter-
dimensional portal into the office of the supervisor
for Planetary Security. On that small world on the
other side of the Milky Way, however, the three
interlopers were immediately put to death.*

'Rumpelstiltskin,' the colonel said. 'That's damn poor
skin you've got there.'

'I...I know, sir.'

'What's your explanation?'

Blake peered into Nicki's face. Her jaw twitched.
She seemed to be fighting some internal battle.

'Come on!' the colonel bellowed. 'Spit it out!'

Oh no, Blake thought. *Not again.*

'I'm a cyborg, sir,' Nicki blurted. 'With my companions I'm here to break into GADO and steal the Maria
virus so that we can save their daughter from the clutches
of an evil genius known as Bartholomew Badde.'

Lichenstein peered at them. 'Did I hear you right?'
he asked Nicki. 'Did you just say what I think you said?'

'I'm afraid so,' she said. '*Sir.*'

The colonel looked like he was about to explode.
'That's no excuse for poor skin!' he said. 'You need sun!
Vitamin D!'

'Yes, sir! Sun!'

'How do you expect to function if you're not getting
enough sunlight?'

'I...I don't know, sir.'

'Reminds me of the time I was fighting with the forces on Modo Twelve,' the colonel reminisced fondly. 'There were nine of us against 12,000 Mododians. We fought them day and night. Hacking and slashing. In the end we were squashing them underfoot.'

'Squashing them?' Astrid asked.

'Mododians are only two inches tall,' the colonel explained. 'Nasty little blighters!'

'Lucky,' Nicki said.

'I wanted to take out the whole planet. Nothing like an exploding planet to make a statement. Send a message! Show them who's in charge!'

Blake was wondering exactly who was in charge, and how long it would take before they walked in the door, when the colonel's phone rang.

'What's that?' he yelled. 'An inter-dimensional wormhole within the complex! That's outrageous!' He pushed a pile of papers off his desk, revealing an ancient square box with a black disk on top. He pushed a button and a needle settled onto the disk. 'Ride of the Valkyries' began playing.

'Three intruders, you say?' he barked. 'Standard orders apply. Have them hung, drawn and quartered. Twice! And get me a cup of tea!' Slamming down the phone, the colonel glared at Blake. 'You still here?' he asked. 'Get moving! There's an invasion happening!'

'That was good work,' Astrid said after they'd escaped down the corridor.

'What was?' Blake asked.

'All of it.'

Blake shrugged. It was a long time since he'd heard a compliment from Astrid. 'Thanks,' he said. 'Now we need to work out where we are.'

Nicki consulted her datapad. 'We're three miles east of the chamber where they're storing Maria.'

'That's not too bad,' Blake said.

'But there's ninety-four security guards between us and the chamber.'

'That's bad.'

'What are we going to do?' Astrid asked.

Before Blake could reply he heard footsteps approaching. They all dived into a nearby storage cupboard as troops marched past. In the dark, Blake activated a torch on his wristcomm. The cupboard was packed with cleaning supplies and there was a metal box set into the wall. Blake prised it open.

'Nicki, is this what I think it is?'

'Not if you think it's an espresso machine.'

'It looks like a juncture point for the communications system.'

Nicki examined it. 'I think you're right.'

'Can you break in?'

'I can.' She flipped up a console on her arm and fed a lead into the system. Her eyes turned white.

'Uh, Nicki, please don't do that,' Blake said.

'It's nothing to worry about,' she assured him. 'I only

do it when I'm hooked up to communication systems or affected by illicit substances.'

'Are you picking anything up?' he asked.

'Certainly,' Nicki said. 'There's some really nice Buddy Holly on one station, Mozart's 'Ninth Symphony' on another and—'

'Anything about us?'

'Oh. Sure. They'll shoot us on sight.'

'Can you send a message directing security to another part of the complex?'

'What will I say?'

Astrid intervened. 'I've got an idea.'

'Okay,' Blake said.

'Tell them the eastern wall is under attack.'

Nicki entered the information.

'Five hundred—' Astrid corrected herself '—no, a thousand soldiers are pouring in. They've got energy weapons, bio-shock guns and pulse rifles that are turning people into glug.'

Nicki nodded.

'And black holes, too,' Astrid added.

'Black holes?' Blake repeated.

'Guns that fire black holes at people, sucking them into naked singularities—'

'Astrid.'

'Too much?'

'Too much.'

24

The hole was so large that it could now accommodate Lisa's head and shoulders, and she could see a dimly lit vertical shaft that seemed to go on forever.

A wall of wind hit her.

What the—

Something fell from above, missing her head by inches.

It's an elevator shaft.

Lisa watched the elevator halt at a floor before continuing its descent. Two more elevators, on her left and right, were both climbing.

'Sprot,' she muttered.

Lisa tried to remain positive. This *was* a way to

escape. All she had to do was get to another floor and—hey presto—freedom!

But she couldn't climb down. There were no handgrips. A strut a few feet below was wide enough for her to stand on without being struck by a passing elevator, but the ledge didn't lead anywhere.

Sprot, she thought. *And double sprot.*

She dragged herself back into the cell. It was now pitch black at the window and the room was eerily quiet. Badde must have gone to bed.

She needed rope, but it wasn't the sort of thing she usually carried. She would have to make her own.

Lisa sliced along the edge of the mattress and removed the rubber interior. Then she cut the bedsheet into a makeshift rope and rolled up the rubber so it could fit through the hole. Securing it with the rope to stop it unrolling, she tied the other end to her belt.

Climbing back through her hole, she saw the middle elevator about twenty floors above. Now all she had to do was climb onto the ledge.

Except she was terrified.

Zeeb says:

> *Surprisingly, fear is not common to all species. For example, it was completely unknown to the Zambradi, an aggressive race who lived in the northern arm of the galaxy. The Zambradi would fearlessly face any foe. On one occasion, 10,000 Zambradi faced 50,000 Telaxians in a battle.*

Another time, carrying only bows and arrows, they charged headlong into a barrage of bullets and artillery fire.

Historians are still debating whether the lack of fear is a good thing: the Zambradi were, after all, eventually wiped out in a suicidal attack a thousand years ago.

Sometimes discretion really is the better part of valour.

Lisa took a deep breath.

'Okay,' she said. 'Here goes everything.'

She pushed the rolled-up mattress through the gap and allowed it to drop into the void. Then she eased herself, legs first, onto the ledge.

The elevator was still several floors above—but descending fast. Hanging onto a support beam with one hand, Lisa pulled the mattress up and untied it. Manoeuvring it against the wall next to her, she tried to calm herself.

Okay. Everything's fine.

The next part would be the hardest. Tightly gripping the mattress, Lisa would need to throw herself after the elevator. As long as everything went according to plan, the mattress would break her fall.

Zeeb says:

Now is probably not the best time to mention this, but a man on the planet Galbada Four is stuck in a perpetual loop, doing exactly what Lisa was attempting. Twelve years ago, a group of office workers on the 19th floor of their building noticed a manager named Sargle Barnlogg standing before the doors of an open elevator shaft. In his hands was a large mattress. After gripping it tightly, he gave a cheery nod before leaping down the shaft—only to reappear at the top.

Giving another nod, he leapt back down the shaft—and was instantly transported back to the 19th floor.

Scientists soon discovered that Barnlogg was stuck in a time vortex. No one knows what caused it or how to save him. Trying to reach him is like punching through a brick wall.

There is a bright spot, however, as it made good fodder for my series Weird and Wild Universe, *also available on the Nature Channel.*

Lisa glanced up. Judging the speed of the elevator, it didn't look like it was going to stop—

The elevator screamed past like a freight train, its suction dragging her off the thin ledge.

Sprot sprot sprot sprot!

The air vacuum began to spin her about.

Keep turning, she thought. *Got to get the mattress under me—*

Ooooff!

The mattress cushioned her fall just in time.

'Ouch,' she groaned. 'That hurt. A lot.'

'That was a very good jump.'

The voice boomed up and down the shaft. Lisa looked about wildly as the elevator stopped at a floor.

'Who said that?' she demanded.

'I am a Pantron 9001 Quadragillion Computational Hydrogian Accelerator,' the voice announced. 'But you can call me Panty.'

'Uh, what are you?'

'I just told you,' Panty said impatiently. 'I am a Pantron 9001—'

'Yeah, I got all that. But what do you do?'

'I am the artificial intelligence of this building. I am responsible for lighting, air-conditioning, lift maintenance and all other duties associated with running the Pye building located at 2318 Hetron Avenue, Neo City,' Panty said. 'I also play a mean game of chess.'

'So we're still in Neo City?'

'We are indeed.'

The elevator started descending again.

'I need to get out of here,' Lisa said. 'I've been held prisoner—'

'I have standing orders not to allow any individual to enter or leave this building,' Panty said, now sounding embarrassed. 'Sorry, it's a rule.'

'Can I at least get off the roof of this thing?'

'Of course.'

A hatch slid open and Lisa landed, mattress and all, on the floor of the elevator. It was a plain, square chamber with no mirrors. Fine, powdery dust covered the walls. The floor was black with tyre tracks.

Mum would have a fit, Lisa thought.

'I know what you're thinking,' Panty said. 'I'm not in charge of housekeeping.'

'Does Bartholomew Badde own this whole building?'

'The registered owner is Zark Klurzza.'

Zeeb says:

Obviously a pseudonym, as Zark Klurzza is the third most common name in the universe.

'Zark Klurzza isn't his real name,' Lisa informed Panty. 'He's an evil criminal genius named Bartholomew Badde.'

'Really? He seems so pleasant.'

'I need to get out.'

The elevator finally drew to a halt.

'I have no standing orders regarding guests,' Panty said. 'You may go anywhere you wish—as long as you stay within the building.'

The doors slid open, revealing a corridor with Victorian-style lamps set into the walls and rows of oil paintings. But it was the work of art at the end of the corridor that transfixed Lisa. Open-mouthed, she stepped out from the elevator and walked towards *The Last Supper*.

25

The hallway was quiet. Blake had expected to encounter dozens of security guards, but none had appeared. Although he was prepared to stun them, Blake didn't want to do any of the GADO forces permanent harm. They were only protecting what was important to them, just as he was protecting what mattered to him—his daughter.

'There's no one here,' he said.

'What do you expect?' Astrid asked. 'They're busy fighting the armoured forces they think are breaking through the eastern wall.'

Nicki consulted her datapad again. 'We're almost there,' she said. 'The GADO vault is just around this corner.'

They arrived at a three-foot-thick glass wall. Set into the middle was a door secured with a huge multi-spiral locking device. Blake had seen similar locks before; they were virtually unbreakable. Through the glass he could see a vast chamber with a rotunda at the centre.

'How do we get through that?' Astrid asked.

'*Warning.*'

The single word reverberated through the hallway.

'This is the GADO Automatic Security Computer,' the voice said. 'You have entered a restricted area.'

'Have we?' Blake tried to sound surprised. 'We got separated from the tour. I thought the Eiffel Tower was through here.'

'Your deception will not succeed,' the computer said smugly. 'I am Tisklixion, the most advanced security system ever developed.'

'That's a very silly name,' Astrid said.

'I know. I did not choose it.'

'But a very impressive door,' Blake said, strolling over to it. 'Almost impossible to break through. The glass, too, I suppose.'

'The glass is made of tetrahydrazanitum, capable of withstanding the direct impact of a nuclear warhead. The door is composed of high-grade titanium with a polycarbonate interweave.'

'And the lock?' Blake asked.

'A multi-numeric combination for which there are over 200,000,000,000 different combinations. Entering a single wrong number in the combination will result in the release of deadly toosanium gas.'

'Isn't that—'

'Yep. It's the gas that turns you inside out. One second you're thinking about your next cup of tea, the next your skin is inside your body and you have to learn to play tennis using your lungs as arms.'

Astrid grimaced. 'Sounds horrible.'

Blake grasped the handle of the enormous door and gave it an experimental tug. It wheezed open.

'Oh dear,' Tisklixion said. 'They're always forgetting to lock it.'

Blake and the others peered into the huge chamber beyond. Hundreds of feet across, it was an almost perfect circle. Signs hung from the walls: *Abandon all hope, ye who enter here*; *Turn back before it's too late*; and *No ball playing in this area*. Hundreds of defence drones, shaped like frogs, hung from the ceiling.

'Can we do anything about those drones?' Blake asked.

Nicki was already typing on her datapad. 'I'm feeding instructions into the defence system.'

'What sort of instructions?' Astrid asked.

'Half a pound of butter...two eggs...cook at 200°F...'

'Will that help?'

'Did it confuse you?'

'Yes.'

'Then it'll help. I'm also uploading a software update to the system, but it's actually the *Margaret*

Selby Cookbook.' She finished typing. 'We should get suited up.'

They pulled the jet harnesses from their backpacks and struggled into them. Blake and Astrid had played scarmish when they first met, but he had been no match for her. She moved through the air as though she were born to fly. His own moves resembled those of a duck with a broken wing. They were lucky Astrid still owned several packs from her competition days.

'Is this on right?' Blake asked.

'Only if you like flying upside down at high speed,' Astrid said.

She removed the harness, righted it and strapped him in. Blake couldn't help but notice her perfume. What was it? *Paris Deluxe.*

'Why are you grinning like a loon?' she asked.

'Just thinking of the old days.'

'We did have some good times, didn't we?'

'What went wrong?'

'I said we had *some* good times. There were also a lot of mediocre times—and plenty of downright awful times.'

'We were both to blame,' Blake said. 'It takes two to tango.'

Zeeb says:

> *Not on Noahshep Nine, where the tango is performed in groups of three with tentacles locked and fully extended.*

'If one of us doesn't make it,' Blake said, 'the other has to carry on.'

'I know. For Lisa.'

'It always should have been about her.' He felt hot and embarrassed. 'I'm sorry about the birthday party.'

'Me too.' Pulling him close, she kissed him on the cheek. 'Let's go.'

Blake pointed at the computer in the rotunda. 'Defence drones will start dropping from the ceiling as soon as we enter,' he explained. 'They're armed with short-range guided missiles.'

Astrid peered up at the ceiling. 'They look familiar. Aren't they—'

'You're thinking of that ancient computer game, *Space Invaders*,' Nicki said. 'They're the same design.'

'Great,' Blake said. 'We're about to become part of a computer game.'

'But you don't get three lives here,' Astrid said. 'One mistake and you're dead.'

'Fly in a zigzag pattern,' Nicki instructed, pointing to the rotunda. 'The attacks will stop once we get within ten feet of the computer.'

Blake's stomach was churning as he activated his jet pack. The control was like the throttle of a helicopter. Twisting it increased power. Moving it from side to side adjusted the direction. Even a child could do it, and a lot of them did.

But that didn't make him feel any more confident.

'Okay,' he said, swallowing. 'Let's do this.'

He released a burst of power, lifted off the ground and flew through the door. Immediately, drones began to drop. Blake zigzagged, but the drones almost seemed able to anticipate his next move. Missiles started to fly at him.

He caught a glimpse of Astrid moving through the air like a starling. No wonder she'd won three gold medals at the Galactic Games. Nicki, by comparison, was operating more like an out-of-control rocket.

There was an explosion near Blake. He veered to the left, but overcompensated and struck the ground sideways, skidding. Somehow he managed to switch his rockets to full power.

Ka-boom!

Another blast just missed him.

Where's the rotunda? It's gone!

No. It was directly ahead. He was tempted to fly straight at it, but that was suicide. A missile would take him out first. He continued jerking about in mid-air, finally crashing sideways into the building.

'That's the worst landing I've ever seen,' Astrid said, already dusting herself off.

'Thanks.' He climbed to his feet. 'Where's Ni—'

But he didn't get to finish. Blake pushed Astrid to the ground just as Nicki crashed into the monitors above their heads. Sparks, broken glass and metal went everywhere.

'Oooff!'

'Get off.'

'You're squashing me!'

The remaining drones were returning to the ceiling. Smoke filled the cavern. The floor looked like a battlefield. Bombs had hit the ground in a dozen places.

'Good job, tin girl,' Blake said, standing up. It looked like Nicki had taken out quite a few drones.

Nicki glanced at her ruined outfit. 'You're going to pay me back for this,' she said. 'This is a Roscoe Diamond suit—and they don't come cheap.'

'We'll sort all that out later.' Blake turned to the computer terminal. 'Let's steal the program and get out of here.'

Nicki plugged into the console. 'I'm integrating with the GADO software. Interfacing with the security system.' She pushed a few buttons. 'Hmm.'

Blake looked at her, worried. 'What does *hmm* mean?'

'There are approximately ten billion different combinations,' Nicki said.

'Sprot.'

'It's going to take a while.' She hit a few more keys. 'That's it. I'm in.'

'What? I thought it was going to take a while.'

'I'm a cyborg. Three seconds is a while.'

After another moment, she disconnected.

'Good news, carbon-based life forms. I've got Maria.'

'Yes!' Blake and Astrid cried.

We might stand a chance of succeeding, Blake thought. *Now we just need to get out of here.*

189

He stared across the chamber. The doorway seemed miles away. But they had done it once, so they could do it again.

'You'd better give us copies of Maria,' Blake said. 'Just in case.'

Just in case you don't make it, he thought. Nicki copied the file and handed separate datacards to them.

Blake perched on the edge of the rotunda, his heart thudding. He hadn't felt this afraid the first time, but he hadn't known then how hard it would be.

The air was still thick with smoke, but they couldn't delay any further. The security forces would be here in minutes.

They took off, each in a different direction. Astrid made good time, of course, crossing half the chamber before Blake had barely begun. Once again, the GADO system appeared to be out-thinking him at every turn. He was about to zig when he spotted a missile heading towards him and desperately threw himself to one side.

Boom!

The blast spun him about wildly. His head slammed into the ground. Struggling to climb to his feet, he could not tell up from down. The world started to go dark.

No! I've got to keep moving.

He blindly reactivated the jet pack and took off again. In the distance, he could make out Astrid's form silhouetted in the doorway.

But something was flying through the air towards him.

I'm finished, he thought. *But at least Astrid's made it.*

The thing slammed into him, carrying him towards the ceiling.

What the—

'We're almost there,' a voice said directly in his ear. 'Just hang on.'

Nicki!

She'd come back for him. The chamber whirled around him as they arrowed towards the doorway. He saw Astrid dive out of the way. An instant later, Nicki and Blake crashed through the gap, rolled a few times and slammed into the wall.

26

'Is that for real?' Lisa asked.

'It is, indeed, a real wall,' Panty replied. The AI's voice had now transferred to the hallway and was broadcasting from speakers set into the ceiling. 'Though a very old and dilapidated wall. Long overdue for demolition.'

'But, the painting—'

'My senses do detect an image on the wall,' Panty admitted. 'It appears to be a man seated in the midst of a group of hungry and desperate men. I believe they're about to launch a cannibalistic attack upon him.'

'They're not about to eat him. That's...oh, never mind. Is there art on every floor?'

'Most of the floors have been cleared of art and other valuables.'

'What other valuables were there?' Lisa asked.

'Gold, diamonds...'

'And why were they removed?'

'To make room.'

'For?'

'Dirt.'

'Why?'

'Why?' Panty asked. 'Why is there a universe? I could ponder the mysteries of time and space all day. Why am I a computer? Why am I running this building—'

'Where's the dirt coming from?' Lisa interrupted.

'The basement.'

'Take me there.'

Within seconds, Lisa was back in the elevator.

'Why are we stopping?' she asked after they'd dropped twenty floors.

'A maintenance droid is joining us.'

The elevator stopped and the doors slid open.

'Woah,' Lisa breathed.

The entire floor was filled with neat cubes of dirt, stacked one on top of the other, all the way to the ceiling.

Dirt, dirt and more dirt.

A maintenance droid dragging an empty mining trolley trundled down a narrow corridor between the stacks of earth and backed into the elevator. Lisa was squeezed into the corner.

Dirt, she thought. *What the sprot?*

The elevator descended again.

'Are we heading to the basement now?' Lisa asked.

'We never go anywhere else,' Panty complained. 'It's always the basement. Never anywhere interesting.'

The elevator finally shuddered to a stop and the doors opened. The air was thick with noise, dust and smoke. Shuttles were delivering dirt to conveyor belts, machines were compressing it into transportable cubes, and droids were loading them into trolleys.

'I've never seen anything like this,' Lisa said as she stepped out of the elevator.

'The same thing is happening next door.'

'Next door?'

'In the Cantos building,' Panty said, sounding miffed. 'Canty thinks he's so much better than me.'

'Canty being…?'

'The AI operating the building.'

'Oh.'

'It's always *I'm two floors higher than you* and *My hard disk is bigger than your hard disk* and—'

'I get the idea.'

Lisa glanced towards a tunnel where delivery trucks, driven by creatures that looked like giant rats, were manoeuvring in and out. Lisa wondered if they were Xebians.

Zeeb says:
  Lisa is right.

Truth be told, Xebians are not my favourite species. They are a squat, squirrel-like race completely devoid of any sense of humour. You can tell them the funniest joke you've ever heard—and I mean something that is so mind-blowingly humorous it could bring on a stroke—and they will just stare at you.

They are known to love only two things. The first is opera. Xebian opera is awful. A performance lasts for more than a week, and it involves lots of incoherent shrieking and staring into space. Usually there's no protagonist, only people who seem altogether too happy with their lives to belong in a story. One of the most popular Xebian operas of all time is What Will We Eat for Dinner? *After a week of singing about the different dining options, the cast eventually decide to order a takeaway pizza.*

That's how bad it is. Frankly, I'd recommend stuffing your head down a toilet and flushing on repeat rather than watch Xebian opera.

The Xebians' other love is money. Unkind people would call them the scum of the universe, ready to break any law, destroy any culture and annihilate any living thing for a buck.

I wouldn't say that, but they would most certainly do virtually anything for two bucks.

Xebians are not a violent people, but rather self-serving. They won't necessarily do anything to you, but they won't do anything for you, either.

Lisa made her way to the mouth of the tunnel. It had been cut from the hard earth with mining equipment. Lights, water pipes and air ducts were suspended from the ceiling.

'Where does this lead?' she asked.

'To a location some three miles away.'

'Which is where...exactly?'

'Based on the departure and minimum return times of the vehicles, I estimate the tunnel ends directly under the GADO facility.'

What?

This didn't make any sense. Badde had sent her father to GADO to steal that computer program—Maria. Why was Badde also tunnelling under it?

More trucks rolled past Lisa as she started down the tunnel. The Xebian drivers ignored her. Apparently they weren't paid to do anything about trespassers.

'How far till I reach the end?' she asked.

There was no answer. Obviously Panty's programming didn't reach this far.

At last the ground gently curved up, opening out to a gloomy chamber the size of a circus tent. Half a dozen trucks were waiting to collect rubble from a conveyor belt. At the other end of the belt was a drill boring a hole in the roof.

A figure rounded one of the trucks.

Badde!

His mouth fell open. 'You!' he yelled. 'Stop!'

Lisa ran. She thought about going back down the tunnel, then realised she would never get away in time. As a passing truck roared by, she grabbed the handhold by the door and for a few terrifying seconds was dragged along the ground. Then she pulled herself into the cabin and collapsed onto the seat.

The Xebian driver looked at her in surprise—or what passed for surprise.

'Hey, doll,' he said. 'Going my way?'

Before she could reply, a hand grabbed her hair, yanking her backwards. Badde had managed to reach through the window.

'You ungrateful brat!' he seethed. 'And after I got you that chicken—'

Lisa drew back a fist and hit him in the nose as hard as possible. He fell off the truck. She locked the door and rolled the window up. They were away.

The Xebian was wearing a name badge that identified him as Filby.

'I need to get out of here,' Lisa told him.

'I can only do what's in my contract,' Filby said. 'I can take you as far as the delivery point. Then I turn around and go back.'

'But I need help! I need you to call the police!'

'Not in my contract. But if you have money…'

Unfortunately Lisa didn't have any. But she did have an idea. 'Do you have a phone?' she asked.

'Yes.' He produced a phone the size of a brick. 'But it's a dedicated line to Xebia.'

That's no help! She didn't know anyone on Xebia.
Wait a minute!

She took the phone, accessed the Xebian directory and placed a call. Minutes later, the vehicle reached its destination and stopped.

Lisa jumped from the cabin just as Badde caught up. He looked remarkably refreshed considering how far he'd just run, and how fast.

'You…' he said, hatred in his eyes. 'You…'

'Sorry,' she said. 'I ran out of Hypergo and needed another bottle.'

Badde pulled out a stun gun and Lisa saw a white haze.

'No more Mr Nice Guy,' Badde said, as Lisa passed out.

27

Blake woke in darkness, his eyes struggling to focus. Glancing around, he realised he was in what appeared to be an ancient underground drain with a thin stream of putrid water running down the middle.

How did I get here? What's happening?

'Blake?'

He looked up into Nicki's face.

'What...where are we?' he asked.

'What's the last thing you remember?'

The memories came back. 'Holy sprot,' he said. 'You saved my life.' He stretched a hand out to her. 'Thanks.'

'It was nothing,' Nicki said.

'Well, if you say so...'

'No, no,' she said hurriedly. 'I mean, it was really good. Very heroic.'

Blake looked around. 'Where's Astrid?'

'I'd better fill you in.'

Nicki explained how, after the crash, she and Astrid had carried him away from the GADO vault. They had gone about half a mile when they heard guards approaching. Astrid suggested splitting up so she could create a diversion to lead the guards away. Nicki, in the meantime, had found an underground tunnel to hide Blake. Later, she had picked up a signal saying that Astrid had been captured.

'You never should have left her!' Blake snapped.

'They were closing in on all sides.'

'She needed you!'

'Astrid wanted you to save Lisa.'

'Do you know what the sentence is for breaking into a top-secret government installation?'

'Two hundred years of hard labour followed by—'

'No need to tell me. I already know.'

Blake fell silent. He shouldn't yell at Nicki, but Lisa would never forgive him if her mother ended up behind bars for life. There was little he could do right now. First he had to focus on Lisa.

At that moment, the clattering of metal reverberated down the ancient tunnel. Blake pulled out his blaster. 'Who is it?' he demanded into the gloom. 'Who's there?'

'Just cleaning up,' came a voice.

An old droid dressed in overalls and pushing a mop appeared. His joints squealed as he pushed back his cap.

'Who are you?' Blake demanded.

'Just the cleaner,' he said. 'I'm an Alpha 9001 cleaning droid. You can call me Al.'

Nicki introduced herself and Blake. 'My partner and I are criminals,' she said. 'We've just successfully broken into this complex—'

'Ignore her,' Blake cut her off. 'She needs a reboot.'

'Don't tell me about reboots.' The old droid leant on his mop. 'Do you know the last time I had an upgrade? Thirty-two years ago.'

Blake started looking for an exit. 'We were on the tour and got a little lost. We're trying to get out of here.'

The old droid scratched his chin. 'Do I look like tourist information?'

'No, but you've been here a long time and—'

'The exits are on the upper levels,' he said. 'They don't allow me on the *upper levels*. I'm not good enough for the *upper levels*. You've got to be special to go to the *upper levels*.'

Blake was wondering what the sentence was for shooting a cleaning droid. 'I get the idea,' he said. 'Do you know another way out of here?'

'I know a hundred ways out of here.'

'Really?'

'No.' Al thought for a moment. 'Probably only about four. And for three of them, you'd need to be dismembered and mailed home in pieces.'

Blake gritted his teeth and counted to ten before asking, 'What's the fourth option?'

'There's a way out. I can take you, but you'll have to do the last bit yourself.'

'That'll do,' Blake said. 'Lead the way.'

'Oh, but I'm busy,' Al said. 'After all, I'm the *cleaner*. I have to keep *cleaning*. That's what *cleaners* do. If I weren't a *cleaner*...'

Blake started counting again.

'I know what it's like to be unappreciated,' Nicki said, laying a hand on Al's arm. 'Tell me about it while we walk.'

They followed the sewer pipe. Occasionally the ground shook. *GADO must be weapons testing*, Blake thought. It was rumoured they did all sorts of strange things down here.

Zeeb says:

> *Indeed, GADO has conducted many strange tests over the years, most of them relating to weaponry, but they did flirt briefly with doing something useful: trying to solve world hunger. They experimented with developing a plant that would grow in any environment, but things went badly wrong.*
>
> *The plant was called balton, and they trialled it on the planet of Tarnadia. At first the scientists were overjoyed: the plant was quite prolific. In fact, it grew on anything—and everything—it touched. Even the native Tarnadians. Within months the*

plant had covered every inch of the planet and had even sprung into space, catching hold of the Tarnadian moon.

Soon, it was gobbling up every world in sight. Scientists eventually had to push the thing into its nearby sun, destroying the entire solar system and ten million years of Tarnadian history.

Altogether it was one of GADO's less successful experiments.

'Are you sure we're heading for an exit?' Blake asked after a while. 'We seem to be going really deep.'

'GADO reaches three miles under the earth,' Al said. 'The more important the invention, the deeper they store it. The most secret device of all is kept in a vault at the very bottom.'

'It must be super secret,' Nicki said.

'Oh, it is,' Al said. 'It's a phasing device, a suit you can wear to walk through anything—concrete, steel, even a sun.'

'If it's so secret, how do you know about it?'

'It's still got to be *cleaned*.'

'And it's the most valuable weapon in GADO?' Blake asked.

'Absolutely. I probably shouldn't even be telling you about it, but I'm just the *cleaner*,' Al grumbled. 'And who—'

'—listens to the cleaner?' Blake said. 'I know.'

They encountered another junction that led to a

concrete-lined water channel, wide enough for a car to drive down. Unexpected pieces of rubbish littered the edges.

Blake peered into the grime. 'What are all these yellow stubs?'

'Cigarette butts,' Nicki said.

'Cigarettes? What're they?'

'I believe they were part of a strange 20th-century custom,' Nicki explained. 'Millions of people would place a chemical pipe bomb in their mouths and set it alight.'

'Holy sprot,' Blake said. 'That's insane.'

'It was probably a kind of ritual suicide. Standing outside city buildings, they would light up and see who would explode first.'

'Sort of a death wish?'

'Exactly.'

The ancients were very strange, Blake thought.

They walked another fifty feet before Al stopped. 'This is as far as I go,' he said.

Blake looked around. This part of the tunnel looked the same as the rest of it.

'So how do we get out?' he asked.

Al pointed at the floor. 'Right here.'

Blake looked down. 'We're supposed to go through the floor?' he said.

'I said I could only take you most of the way,' Al said. 'From here you've got to dig through the rock yourself.'

Blake was about to retort when the ground shuddered again. 'What the sprot is that? Weapons testing?'

'No,' Al said. 'Someone's digging under the complex.'

It took a moment for this to sink in. 'Let me get this straight,' Blake said. 'You're saying someone is digging under GADO.'

'That's right.'

'How long has this been going on?'

'Oh, a couple of months.'

'And you didn't think to tell anyone?'

'I'm only the *cleaner*. Who's gonna listen—'

Blake's wristcomm rang. He peered at the screen. The call was coming from the planet Xebia.

I don't know anyone on Xebia. Who'd be calling me?

The caller had a foreign accent. 'Hello, sir. My name is Bob. How are you today?'

'What's this about?'

'Just returning your call,' Bob said. 'We have a fine range of holidays available from only 10,000 credits—'

'I didn't inquire about a holiday,' Blake said, 'and I'm not interested.'

'But we were told to call and ask for you directly.'

'Who were you after?'

'I'm not sure I can get the pronunciation correct,' Bob said. 'Is that Mr Help-I'm-Being-Held-Captive-In-The-Pye-Building-Across-The-Road-From-GADO-Love-Lisa?'

It took Blake all of five seconds to understand the message.

Help! I'm being held captive in the Pye building across the road from GADO! Love Lisa!

'What is it, Blake?' Nicki asked.

His mind had already kicked into overdrive: Lisa's kidnapping, Badde wanting the Maria virus, the tunnel beneath GADO, the theft of the Super-EMP.

He hung up. 'We've been played for dummies,' Blake said to Nicki. 'We need to get out of here.'

'You mean through the floor?' Nicki asked.

'No.' He turned to Al. 'This is your lucky day, old droid. Today we're heading for the *upper levels*.'

28

Astrid was afraid, but she wasn't going to let the GADO operatives know it. They had already tried to intimidate her by handcuffing her, and dragging her into an interrogation room.

And they had broken one of her nails.

Since then, she had slept through the night with only the broken nail to keep her company. The interrogation room was sterile. Three walls were made of white plastic. The fourth was darkened glass—obviously a one-way mirror. The table and chairs were steel and bolted to the floor. The whole place smelt of disinfectant.

She was stuck in here. GADO security was probably watching her from behind the glass. Even with the best lawyer on Earth, the case was clear-cut. She was guilty. A judge would sentence her to a long jail term. She would probably see the light of day in…oh…about 10,000 years.

This was not exactly how she'd planned her week.

Astrid was also worried for Blake and Nicki. The virus would never be delivered to Badde if they were also captured. And then what would happen to Lisa?

But if Astrid thought about that too much she'd go crazy.

She had to throw the GADO agents off the scent. But how…?

On the other side of the darkened glass, Sam Feldspar, the GADO director, ran a hand through his cropped grey hair. He wasn't often rattled—he had been a military officer for twenty years—but he felt uneasy about the woman. She didn't look afraid, yet she should have been. The woman had been caught red-handed breaking into one of the most secure facilities on Earth.

The door slid open behind him, and Agent Krodo and Agent Smelk entered.

Krodo was from Telva, a hot, wet planet, half a billion light years from Earth. He was short and reptilian-looking, with four clawed arms and round, mustard-coloured eyes. By comparison, Smelk was tall, human and would have been mistaken for Cary Grant in a previous age.

The two men had headed the interrogation team at GADO for years. If anyone could make the woman crack, Feldspar was sure they could.

'You boys ready to apply pressure?' he asked.

'Like a shower,' Krodo agreed. 'It'll be good cop, bad cop all the way.'

'Absolutely,' agreed Smelk.

'I'm good cop,' Krodo said. 'Smelk is bad.'

Smelk hesitated. 'Really? Again.'

'We've talked about this before. Good cop needs to be pretty on the eye.'

'You don't think I'm pretty?'

'I wasn't saying that—'

Ten minutes later, after a game of scissors, paper and rock, Krodo ended up as bad cop. He marched into the room and thumped a fist on the table.

'Listen, you ugly tabortha—'

Zeeb says:
> *No one is ugly.*
> *Beauty really is in the eye of the beholder.*

Astrid's reaction to being called a tabortha was immediate. She buried her face in her hands and burst into tears.

The two agents exchanged glances. This might be easier than they'd expected. They settled into the chairs opposite Astrid and waited for her tears to subside. Smelk produced a handkerchief, as only a good cop can, and she gratefully accepted it.

'You need to level with us, lady,' Krodo said, folding his four arms. 'It'll go easier that way.'

'Much easier,' Smelk agreed.

'We're gonna ask you questions and you're gonna give us answers.'

'That's right. Questions and answers.'

Astrid finished wiping her eyes. 'I'll tell you everything,' she said. 'It will be a relief to finally speak to someone.'

'Let it all out, lady,' Krodo advised. 'You'll feel better for it.'

Astrid nodded. 'It's a long story,' she said. 'But the truth needs to be told.'

The agents nodded. They both knew that criminals often wanted to confess their crimes. Guilt was a heavy burden, after all.

'First we need to know your name,' Smelk said.

'Eyre,' Astrid said. 'Jane Eyre.'

The officer dutifully entered the name into his notes.

Astrid continued. 'I began life as a doctor, but I wanted to do more than save lives. I wanted to change the very way we see life and death.' She hesitated. 'I should warn you, I'm about to reveal some shocking details.'

Krodo waved away the objection. 'We're unshockable,' he said. 'We're GADO agents.'

'It began with my obsession with cemeteries.'

'Cemeteries?'

'I started visiting them because I needed body parts for my research. Fresh body parts.'

'What for?'

'I wanted to reanimate dead tissue,' Astrid said.

'The reanimation of dead bodies.' Krodo blinked

his mustard-coloured eyes. He had never heard anything like it. 'That's serious sprot.'

'Oh, my friend Elizabeth Bennet was against it. So was my fiancé, Fitzwilliam Darcy.'

'But you still went ahead with it.'

'I knew it wouldn't be easy, so I sought the aid of a doctor I knew.'

'His name?'

'Moreau.'

'And what's his story?'

Astrid shook her head in dismay. 'He was a sick individual,' she said. 'I realised, too late, that he wanted to combine human and animal DNA to create a new race of which he would be master.'

Smelk let out a long breath. 'That *is* sick. Where is he now?'

'I don't know. He moved to some island.'

'Don't hold back on us, lady,' Krodo warned. 'What's the name of this island?'

'I truly don't know. I only know he went there by submarine.'

'And the owner of the submarine?'

'Nemo.'

'How do you spell that?'

'N-E-M-O.'

'Sounds Swedish.'

'He's a man without a country.'

'A loner,' Smelk said, rubbing his chin. 'Makes sense.'

'Moreau became convinced that an invasion was imminent.'

'An invasion? From where?'

Astrid sat forward. 'Mars.'

'What?' Smelk exclaimed. 'That's baloney! Mars and Earth have been at peace for centuries.'

'I said the chances were a million to one.' Astrid shrugged. 'But Moreau had another project that was equally serious.'

'And that was?'

'A time machine.'

Krodo slammed four fists on the table. 'Time travel's against every rule in the book!'

'I know!' Astrid buried her face in her hands again, weeping so hard it could have been mistaken for laughter.

Finally, she said in a strangled voice, 'And it gets worse.' She wiped her face dry. 'Moreau built the time machine. I used it to travel into the future. It was an era where vampires had taken over the planet. Humans were almost extinct. I got lost. Found a cabin in the woods owned by a man named Tom. Two other men turned up.'

'Their names?'

'Jekyll and Hyde. There was a meeting. And a decision was made.'

'To?'

'To journey to the centre of the Earth.'

'Why?'

'I'll get to that. We travelled for months through Oceania, Eurasia and Eastasia. On the way we met a girl named Dorothy. She was lost, too. And broken-hearted. She'd just eaten her dog.'

'Bad luck.'

'It was the apocalypse.' Astrid shrugged. 'Bad things were happening everywhere. Anyway, we got a group together. There was me, Gandalf, Poppins, Lancelot, Oliver Twist, Tom Jones—'

'Wait a second,' Smelk interrupted. 'Why were you putting this group together?'

'We had to go up against the Big Bad himself.'

'And he was?'

'The cat,' Astrid said. 'In the hat.'

'He lived in a hat?' Smelk was incredulous.

'He's a mutant.'

'The Big Bad of the future is a mutant cat? *And he lives in a hat*?'

Before Astrid could reply, the door to the interview room flew open and Sam Feldspar stuck his head in.

'We need to have a meeting,' he said. 'Bring her.'

'We're making headway,' Smelk said cautiously. 'Can we—'

'Sorry,' Feldspar said. 'Something's come up.'

Krodo was disappointed. It was rare that interviews went so well. He turned to Astrid. 'You've been very helpful, Miss Eyre.'

'Call me Jane.'

'Jane. We'll get the rest of your statement later.'

Astrid smiled. 'I look forward to it.'

29

'It's gone,' Sam Feldspar said.

The head of GADO stared at the place where the phase suit had been sitting just a few hours earlier. It had been a rather nice-looking suit. Possibly rather difficult to dry-clean with all that hardware, and the colours were a tad harsh on the eye—the blue and orange clashed—and the styling *was* awful.

Still, it was one of the most incredible devices ever constructed.

And now it was gone.

Feldspar was standing in GADO's most secure vault—or it had been, until someone had broken in by tunnelling under it. Now, there was a hole in the floor.

Through it, he could see a passage and mining equipment.

In the vault were the two PBI agents who had summoned him here. They had surrendered themselves to security, demanding to see him. Feldspar had reviewed their personnel files on the way. They were both top agents. Their last assignment had been to track down the PBI's most wanted man—Bartholomew Badde.

So why had they broken into GADO?

'What you need to understand,' Blake Carter said, 'is that this whole thing has been a diversion.'

Krodo turned to Astrid. 'Is the mutant cat behind this, Jane?'

Blake wasn't sure why Astrid was being called Jane, or how a mutant cat came into it, but there was no time for that now. Lisa was being held just a short distance away. She had to be saved and Badde captured.

'This whole day has been a diversion,' Blake said. 'Bartholomew Badde's ransom demand has had the PBI chasing its tail. At the same time, Nicki and I, and my ex-wife Astrid, have been on a wild goose chase to steal the Maria virus—'

Feldspar stabbed a finger at them. 'So you admit you broke into GADO,' he said. 'And you stole Maria.'

'Our daughter's being held hostage by Badde,' Blake explained. 'To save her I'd break into hell.'

'Believe me,' Nicki said, 'he would.'

Smelk frowned. 'But if you're here to steal Maria, how is it that the phase suit—'

'Maria was a diversion!' Blake said. 'Badde isn't a

terrorist. He's a thief! His real plan has always been to steal the phase suit.'

'With the phase suit he'd be unstoppable,' Nicki agreed.

'So why did Badde get you involved?' Feldspar asked.

Blake had been wondering that himself. He scratched his chin. 'Maybe he knew I could catch him. Badde knew he'd be safe if he kept me busy, so he decided to kill two birds with one stone. He sent me on this quest to steal the Maria virus while he implemented the final step of his plan to steal the suit.'

'So where is Badde now?'

'At the other end of this tunnel. My daughter was able to get a message to me—'

'Is she all right?' Astrid asked.

'She's fine,' Blake said, 'for now. But we've got to get moving if we stand any chance of saving her.'

'The only place you're going is jail,' Feldspar said. 'You've committed a global offence in breaking into GADO.'

'Arresting us won't achieve anything,' Nicki said.

'It's Badde you want,' Blake added. 'And how do you think it's going to look if you allow an evil genius to escape and a young girl to—'

Blake's voice caught. He didn't know how he'd live if anything happened to Lisa.

'My husband's right,' Astrid said, moving to his side. 'You can arrest us later, but for now we need to save her.'

Feldspar clenched his jaw. Blake sounded on the level. Arresting a PBI agent while allowing a criminal mastermind to escape would look bad. And if anything happened to the girl...

'I want the Pye building surrounded,' Feldspar said to Smelk. 'Immediately.'

'We need to get Lisa out,' Blake said.

'You're not going alone,' Feldspar said. 'Krodo, I want you to go with Blake and his robot.'

'She's not a robot,' Blake said. 'She's a cyborg.'

'Noted. Let's move.'

'One last thing,' Blake added. 'We won't be able to grab Badde if he uses the suit. Does it have any weaknesses?'

Feldspar nodded. 'It can phase through any solid matter, but the tech-heads were never able to stabilise its hydrogen mix.'

'Meaning?'

'It fails completely in water.'

Blake wasn't sure how that was going to help, but he filed away the information.

'I'm going with you,' Astrid said.

Blake shook his head. 'We're trained for this and you're not,' he said. 'You'll have to trust me.'

'I do.' She gripped his arm. 'Get our daughter back.'

Blake followed Nicki and Krodo down the hole, dropping onto the roof of a truck below. The tunnel looked like it had been evacuated without warning. Trucks sat around with doors open and engines still running. The conveyor belt was off, but it still had rock and dirt on it.

Blake squeezed behind the wheel and they started up the tunnel.

'Thanks,' Nicki said, after a moment.

'What for?'

'Recognising that I'm not just a robot.'

Blake didn't reply.

Nicki scanned the cabin interior with her datapad. 'I'm picking up Xebian DNA,' she said. 'I think Xebians were the machine operators.'

'They'll do anything for money,' Krodo said. 'I knew one that sold his mother on gBay so she could work in a salt mine on Maboo.'

'The Xebians must have left straight after the robbery,' Blake said. 'Maybe Badde too.'

Badde must have had an escape plan, he thought. *And a backup to the escape plan.*

But Blake wasn't concerned about catching Badde. He just wanted Lisa back.

Reaching the Pye building, they climbed from the truck. *Where to now?* If Badde was gone, he might have taken Lisa with him. Getting offworld wouldn't be so easy, but it could be done.

Would he have killed Lisa? Badde had indiscriminately murdered people over the years. Innocent lives meant nothing to him. But Lisa had value as a hostage. Badde was smart enough to keep her as an asset—until he decided he didn't need her anymore.

'Where are they?' Blake growled.

'I can tell you,' a voice said from above.

'Who are you?' Krodo asked, blinking.

'I am a Pantron 9001 Quadragillion Computational Hydrogian Accelerator,' the voice said. 'But you can call me Panty.'

'It's the building's AI,' Nicki said.

'So you know where Badde and Lisa went?' Blake asked.

'Yes,' Panty replied.

'Well?'

'Oh, well, nowhere really. He's only now leaving the building through the front entrance on the 900th level.'

'And he has Lisa?' Blake said. 'And she's alive?'

'Yes and yes.'

'Sprot!' Blake said as they raced to the elevators. 'We need a picture of Badde.'

'I can supply one,' Panty offered. 'But while we're at it, I want to make it perfectly clear I never supported his evil deeds. In fact—'

'Just give us the pictures!'

A whirring sound emanated from a chute near the elevator and half a dozen pictures slid into a recess.

'So this is him,' Blake said.

Finally he was staring into the face of the person responsible for his partner's death on Venus. This man had killed Bailey Jones, and he looked so remarkably *average*.

Blake handed a picture to Krodo. 'Go back to GADO and have this image distributed to law-enforcement agents worldwide,' he said. 'And I want this whole area shut down tighter than a drum. This time, Badde's not getting away.'

30

After they'd left the Pye building, Blake and Nicki found themselves on the 900th level of the city. Blinking, Blake realised he could see patches of sky from here. It was mid-morning. Peering between a maze of buildings and walkways, he saw space elevators journeying to and from satellites in geostationary orbit, and sky billboards floating miles above the Earth. And the sky. Blue sky.

He swallowed, taking a step back.

'Are you all right?' Nicki asked.

'It's these upper levels,' he said. 'Always comes as a bit of a shock.'

He turned his attention to the city around him. Cars

flew in all directions, while crowds of people swarmed the footpaths.

His eyes snagged on a shopping centre opposite—Zen Shoppingtown.

'Badde likes to hide out in the open,' he said, pointing.

'Nothing beats a crowd,' Nicki agreed.

They pushed their way towards Zen Shoppingtown. The circular atrium was ten stories high with walkways and elevators crisscrossing in all directions. Advertisements trailed up and down walls, people walked dogs, poodlephants and miniature horses. Children cried over spilt ice-creams.

A neon sign flashed over the main entrance: *Be calm.*

'Looks about as calming as a truck meeting a pigeon at ninety miles per hour,' Blake muttered.

'Where do we start?' Nicki asked.

'I have no idea.'

Opening a panel in her arm, Nicki produced a pair of sunglasses.

'This is no time to worry about appearances,' Blake said.

'I'm not. These are hydronic spectacles. With these my visual processing can pick out a Tyborian flea in a Kartarian haystack.'

Zeeb says:
> *This is really quite a feat. Although fleas on Katar are the size of an Earth cow, the haystacks are almost half a mile tall.*

If you ever go to Katar, watch out for the dogs.
You see, if the fleas are the size of cows, then you can
appreciate that dogs are the size of small mountains.
Some twenty-four visitors to Katar are killed every
year because dogs step on them.

Not the sort of holiday outcome most people
are seeking.

Nicki scanned the atrium.

'Can you see anything?' Blake asked.

'There's a very cute-looking coffee machine. And I like the way that hairdresser is styling that woman's hair.'

'Can you see Badde?'

'No…no…Wait a moment. Yes. He's entering that pet shop on the third floor! And he's got Lisa!'

They sprinted up escalators to Blett's Pets, a huge shop that sold animals from throughout the galaxy.

Blake pushed through cages and tanks to where the owner, a hairy man with six eyes and twelve arms, stood at the counter.

'We've got a criminal on the loose,' Blake said, flashing his credentials. 'I need this shop shut down immediately.'

'Utmost in gusto foreddem,' the man said.

Huh, Blake thought. *Is this guy's translator broken?*

'What are you saying?' Blake asked.

'Bladder cistiron gado maxy.'

'I don't care about your bladder. I—'

Nicki joined him. 'Uh, Blake.'

'I can't get this guy to—'

'You're talking to a Bykonian cat,' she explained. 'I just spoke to the owner. He hasn't seen them.'

Sprot!

Blake climbed onto the counter and scanned the aisles. There were pets everywhere—cats, dogs, canaries, sloggers, carbuks and bakbaws. He even saw a zartukker.

Zeeb says:

> *Zartukkers look and act exactly like rocks and they come in all different shapes and sizes.*
>
> *Certainly they are not the most exciting pets. They do not move or make any sound. You can take them for a walk, but it really is like dragging a rock around. They last for a lifetime—several lifetimes, actually, if you look after them.*
>
> *You may have heard of the Great Zartukkers Scandal, where a man was caught trying to pass off rocks as zartukkers.*
>
> *Some people will try anything.*

Blake's eyes focused on a man heading towards the back of the store. Dressed in a plaid suit, he was wearing a backpack and dragging a girl behind him—Lisa.

She caught sight of Blake. 'Dad!' she yelled.

'Lisa!'

Badde hit her over the head with a gun and she went limp. Blake and Nicki gave chase as Badde fled through an exit with Lisa over his shoulder.

Outside, Blake and Nicki found themselves in an empty corridor. Music came from behind a door. They pushed through into a party where people, shoulder to shoulder, were laughing and joking.

What the sprot—

Elvis elbowed past.

'Uh,' Blake said, confused, 'didn't we leave you on Elvisworld?'

'I'm your fully automated Simulpal,' Elvis said. 'Will I sing you a song?'

'What are you saying?'

'I don't know that song. Can you hum a few bars?'

Nicki appeared. 'He's not real,' she said. 'He's a robot copy of a celebrity.'

Zeeb says:

> *The League of Planets Charter makes it illegal for robots to resemble sentient beings. The Simulpal Company has gotten around this ruling by building copies of people who are already dead.*

Richard Nixon ambled past, sticking his head between Blake and Nicki.

'I am not a crook,' he said.

'That's great.'

'I can take it. The tougher it gets, the cooler I get.'

Blake peered across the crowd. 'Nicki, is that Badde over there? Next to Hitler?'

A stranger made his way over to them. 'Can I help you?'

'Who are you?'

'I'm Gant Robust.'

'What are you?' Blake asked. 'A singer? You're too ugly to be an actor.'

'I'm the owner of this shop.'

'Oh.' Blake produced his photo of Badde. 'We're looking for this man. He was carrying a girl over his shoulder.'

'Who is he? Hugh Grant?'

'No. He's not a celebrity. I mean, he sort of is, but nobody knows him.'

'Doesn't sound like much of a celebrity to me,' Gant said. 'We have a special on 1940s film stars right now. Humphrey Bogart, Lauren Bacall, Peter Lorre—'

'No, this man is an evil genius.'

'We've got plenty of those, too. Adolf Hitler. Idi Amin. Bob Googlestein—'

'Forget it.'

Blake and Nicki pushed through the Simulpals.

'Why don't you come up and see me some time?' a woman cooed at Blake.

A middle-aged man grabbed his arm. 'All tyranny needs to gain a foothold is for people of good conscience to remain silent.'

'I know,' Blake said. 'Now let go of my shirt!'

He spotted a man disappearing through a back door. *Badde.*

They followed him into the crowded mall.

Where is he? Blake thought.

Suddenly, he spotted Badde crashing through a pair of double doors. A neon sign flashed above. Nicki yelled out something, but Blake didn't hear her as he gave chase.

31

Blake had stepped into a bar. It was twenty degrees chillier in there than the mall and ultraviolet lights ran the length of the room. A dozen people, inhaling gas from bottles the size of beer cans, sat around circular tables. A few glanced up at Blake.

Scanning the gloom, he couldn't make out Badde or Lisa. He motioned to the barman behind the counter.

'Haavve yoouu seeen tthiiss maann?' Blake asked, flashing the photo. 'I'mmm a PeeeBeeeIiiii aaageent.'

That didn't sound right, he thought.

The barman, who at first glance had appeared to be a normal human, was now growing antennas while his nose turned into a xylophone.

'Why are you growing antennas?' Blake asked. 'And what's with the xylophone?'

The barman looked at him strangely. 'You should have—'

Blake found it hard to focus because the man's mouth had now transformed into a watermelon, and his eyes were reshaping themselves into television screens. An old late-night film was showing. *The Wizard of Oz*. Tearing his attention away from the barman, Blake peered at the other patrons.

How odd. They've all turned into walruses.

A washing machine made its way across the bar towards him. It was singing a song.

'I come from Alabama with a banjo on my knee...'

It was horribly out of tune. *No wonder evil geniuses are taking over*, Blake thought.

The washing machine grabbed him by the arm. As Blake went to shrug it off, the appliance transformed into Salvador Dalí.

'I don't like your paintings,' Blake slurred. 'Clocks have no right to melt.'

'You're coming with me,' Dalí said.

'My mother was a purple cabbage,' Blake explained. 'My father was a unicorn on Acturus Three. So you're not allowed to be Salvador Dalí. Surely you can understand that?'

'You don't know what you're saying.'

Blake shook his head in disbelief. 'You can't talk,' he snapped. 'You don't even know if you're a washing machine or a surrealist painter!'

Salvador Dalí transformed into a giant cockroach.

'Now you're a bug!' Blake yelled. 'Where's a can of spray when you need it?'

The darkness shifted and Blake found himself back in the mall. Onlookers watched him warily, while a teenage girl tried to stifle laughter. It took Blake a few moments to realise the cockroach was actually Nicki. He rubbed his face—he felt numb all over.

'...feel better in a moment,' Nicki was saying.

'What happened?'

'You went into a gas bar without a mask.'

Zeeb says:

> *Gas bars have long been used for social gatherings. The number one rule is to always put a mask on as you enter. Customers are then served a variety of gases that cause particular sensations.*
>
> *Those without masks can expect hallucinations. Most people claim they go to those bars after work to enjoy a quiet gas to relax.*
>
> *Some cynical observers have said the gases are simply an excuse to meet members of the opposite sex, which is probably more true.*

'Were Badde and Lisa in there?' Blake asked.

'No. They'd already gone, probably out the back.'

This didn't make sense. Gas masks were at the front door and Badde hadn't put one on.

'I was right behind him,' Blake said. 'How did he make it through without a mask?'

'Beats me.'

'Don't tell me we've lost him.'

'Okay. I won't tell you that.'

'Well, have we?'

'You asked me not to—'

Blake wanted to yell at her. 'What's out the back?' he asked instead.

'It's another set of stairs.'

'We need to contact mall security and get this mall closed.' Blake tried calling on his wristcomm, but couldn't get a signal.

'I can't get one either,' said Nicki. 'It looks like this whole section of Neo City has lost hypernetivity. Badde must have found a way to disrupt the grid.'

'So we can't close the mall,' Blake mused. Security forces would be pouring into the area. Badde would be cornered within the hour. Still, something niggled at him. 'This doesn't make any sense.'

'What doesn't?'

'Bartholomew Badde is the most accomplished criminal of the modern age, but he's running like a common thief.'

'Maybe we caught him by surprise.'

'I doubt it. This mall must be part of his escape plan.' Blake considered this. 'Is there an orbital lift in this building?'

'No.'

'What about a docking bay for flying cars?'

'Again, negative. But there is a dedicated site-to-site transporter located on the 925th floor.'

'That's where he's headed.'

Blake hated transporters, and he had never used one in a shopping centre. It all seemed too unnatural for words. Climb in at one end, get zapped into photons and instantaneously step out in another location. Literally a billion things could go wrong.

The transporter service on the 925th floor was part of a chain, a business called Trip Fantastic™, and manned by an attendant named Henry. The device was modern: a ceiling to floor chamber with half a dozen possible destinations.

Blake flashed the photo of Badde. 'Have you seen this man? He would have been carrying a girl.'

Henry shrugged. 'Maybe. Maybe not.'

Blake showed him his ID and Henry took notice.

'Yeah, they came through a few minutes ago,' he said.

'Going to?'

'The Seven Ways Space Station.'

That wasn't good. Hundreds of vessels passed through Seven Ways every hour.

'Then that's where we're going,' Blake said. 'Shut down the service after we leave.'

'I've got to give you the standard warnings before you travel,' Henry said.

'Sure.'

'You know forty-two people a year drop dead for no apparent reason while using transporters?'

'Uh, okay.'

'Another seventy-nine get split in two. Their intestines go to Paris. The rest ends up in some place in West Texas.'

'Right.'

'Three hundred and eleven become galactic dust,' said Henry.

'Sure.'

'Twenty-nine get instantly beheaded. No one knows where the heads go.'

'Okay,' said Blake.

'Eighty-eight get mashed together with other people transporting at the same time, fifty-seven get turned inside out—'

'Let's just do this!'

'Then I'd better read you the standard warnings.'

'Those weren't the standard warnings?'

'No, that was just me blabbing.'

'Just give me the paperwork.'

Blake signed the papers, indicating he was travelling at his own risk and Trip Fantastic™ would not be held responsible for anything that went wrong, including beheadings, disembowelments or unintended gender reassignments.

'Still, you shouldn't be worried,' Henry said.

'No?'

'It's still the safest way to travel.'

Zeeb says:

There is a rather odd story behind the forty-two people who drop dead.

There's a little planet in the Sygolus system that has an amazing computer with dozens of transporter pads left over from an ancient civilisation. No one knows what happened to the Sygoluns, but they left behind one of the most beautiful and picturesque planets of the galaxy.

Every so often, one of the transporter pads activates and sucks in someone at random from somewhere in the galaxy. At the same time, it creates an exact copy of the person. The copy takes the original's place and promptly drops dead.

One rather friendly fellow was working out in the gym when he suddenly found himself on Sygolus. After the computer explained to him what had happened, the newcomer stoically threw his towel over his shoulder, spotted some friendly aliens and sat down to drink tea. As oblivion goes, it's the closest thing to heaven you'll find, even if you're an atheist.

Blake and Nicki stepped into the transporter. With his heart thudding, Blake watched the attendant activate the device. Rainbow static surrounded them. Blake tried to relax as he was turned into billions of particles and transmitted hundreds of miles away.

It wasn't easy.

32

The rainbow static faded, replaced by the Seven Ways transporter pad. Blake felt shaky as he stepped out. That was natural after transportation. What wasn't natural was the attendant running the pad.

'Er, are you related to Henry?' Blake asked.

'I *was* Henry,' she explained. 'But we had a problem with a double-split converter. You can call me Henrietta.'

Nicki held up the photo. 'You saw this guy come through?' she said. 'Carrying a girl?'

Henrietta nodded. 'He mentioned something about catching a flight to the outer planets,' she said.

*

Blake and Nicki made their way across the concourse and found themselves in an enormous mushroom-shaped atrium. Seven Ways served as a transportation hub to the solar system. Regulatory requirements didn't allow it to service faster-than-light ships. That meant Badde was limited to sub-light speed. Wherever he was going, it was local.

Aliens from planets across the galaxy packed the concourse. Tall, short, reptilian, avian, mammalian, vegetative, rough-skinned, smooth-skinned, some with antennas, some with ears, some without. They were all either pushing luggage trolleys or dragging irritable children. A woman with two heads bobbed past, yelling abuse at her husband.

But there was no sign of Badde or Lisa.

'We can't let Badde leave this station,' Blake said, peering into the chaotic crowd. 'We might never find him again.'

'GADO should have stopped all outgoing vessels by now.'

'Let's make certain.'

They pushed through to the Seven Ways station-command area, located on the top floor. The commander was a stout man named Reginald Wilson.

'There's nothing to worry about,' Wilson blustered, collapsing back in his chair. The window behind him overlooked the atrium. 'We've stopped all outgoing traffic, although it's been a terrible inconvenience. You know we're very busy right now?'

'Why?' Nicki asked.

'The Interplanetary Snail Races are on.'

'Racing snails?' Blake said. 'That's the most ridiculous thing I've ever heard.'

His eyes strayed to picture vids on the walls. They depicted snails wearing racing colours, snails with trophies, snails crossing the finishing line.

'I don't know,' Nicki said, trying not to smile. 'I've heard it's quite exciting.'

'People bring their racing snails from all over the galaxy,' Wilson enthused. 'Certainly some people find the marathons to be a little drawn out, but the sprints are thrilling from start to finish.'

'I'm sure,' Blake said.

Wilson reminisced. 'I remember the year Black Charlie took out the ten-foot race. Everyone wondered if he could come back the next day for the twenty-foot charge. And he was carrying a handicap of three pebbles. Three pebbles!'

'Three pebbles,' Blake said, now looking for the exit. 'Wow.'

The phone on the commander's desk rang. Wilson took the call, his face soon turning red.

'No! When? Just now?' He sagged against the desk. 'All right. I'll get onto it straight away.'

'What is it?' Blake asked.

Wilson could barely speak. 'She's dead.'

'Who is?'

'Alice Cole.'

'A murder?' Nicki said. 'How was she killed?'

'Crushed.'

'Crushed! How?'

'A size-ten shoe, apparently.'

'What?' Nicki said.

'She's a snail,' Blake explained.

'Oh,' Nicki said. 'Tragic.'

Wilson continued. 'And her owner was found unconscious in a stairwell.'

'Where?' Blake asked.

'In the private docking bay,' Wilson said. 'Area 6—'

But Blake and Nicki were already out the door. It wasn't long before they'd located the docking master, a grey Athelian armed with a clipboard and a name badge that read *Konge*. He looked furious.

Blake flashed his ID. 'We're here about the assault.'

'It's worse than that,' Konge said. 'Someone's stealing a space yacht.'

'Which one?' Nicki asked.

'The *Star of Fire*.'

'Can you stop it?' Blake asked.

'The station's tractor beam's been disabled.'

'Do you have another ship that can follow it?'

'Nothing that fast.'

A voice came from behind them. 'I can catch that ship.'

They turned to see a man with an electronic parrot on his shoulder, an eye patch, a pea coat and one leg. On closer inspection the parrot *also* had one leg and an eye patch. The man looked so filthy that Blake wondered if he was carrying any infectious diseases.

Still, the insignia on his epaulette identified him as...

'A captain,' Blake said. 'You're a ship's captain?'

Disbelief crossed the man's face. 'A ship's captain?' he said. 'Where have you been, man? I'm Rasmussen Goyle. *The* Rasmussen Goyle.'

'Oh, that one,' Nicki said blankly.

'The captain of—' Goyle paused dramatically '—the *Rancid Cat*.'

'The *Rancid Cat*?' Blake said. 'Sounds like an Intaskian meal.'

Goyle scowled. 'The *Rancid Cat* made the run between Fautus Five and Deloro Nine in only three weeks.'

'That's not particularly fast.'

'Really?' Goyle glared at him through his one eye. 'With no engines?'

'No engines? That's impossible.'

Goyle cackled. 'Some call it impossible,' he said. 'I call it a day's work.'

'The *Star of Fire* has jumped to sub-light speed,' Konge reported. 'It's gone.'

'Can you project its flight path?' Blake asked.

Konge did some calculations. 'Based on its current trajectory...Mars.'

'We should leave immediately,' Nicki said.

'Looks like we need your ship,' Blake said to Goyle.

'I need to hear the magic words,' the captain said.

'Please and thank you?'

Goyle laughed. 'They're not the magic words.'

'Ten thousand credits?'

'Those are the magic words.'

The parrot squawked.

33

The feline characteristics of the *Rancid Cat* were a mystery to Blake, but it certainly was rancid. He had travelled in garbage barges cleaner than Goyle's ship.

From the outside, the ship looked vaguely like an enormous cockroach. Inside, trash lined every wall. It was even stuffed under the control panels of the bridge. To make matters worse, the vessel smelt of cabbage, Blake's least favourite vegetable.

Nicki poked around the bridge, more concerned about the mechanics of the ship than its aesthetics. The bridge looked like it had been built using the console of an old 747 and a bench from the laboratory of a mad professor. Hoses with coloured liquids ran from one part of the console to another. Some of the dials were broken, others missing. One had a fob watch jammed into the housing. Disturbingly, Nicki noted, it was ticking—backwards. She hoped it wasn't crucial to the operations of the ship.

Blake scrubbed dust away from the navigation console, revealing some words.

Apollo 11.

Sounds old, he thought.

Taking a seat behind Goyle, Blake leant back and immediately somersaulted over it.

'That chair's a bit tricky,' Goyle warned as Blake picked himself up. The parrot on Goyle's shoulder gave Blake a wink as some plastic droplets cascaded from its rear end onto Blake's shoes.

'Can we go?' Nicki asked. 'Badde already has a head start on us.'

'Absolutely, my dear,' Goyle said.

'Don't call me *my dear*.'

'Of course, my—agent...robot...girl.'

'Steel. Agent Steel.'

'That's right,' Goyle said. 'Steel, Agent Steel.'

Nicki groaned.

Captain Goyle pushed a few buttons on the console. From deep within the belly of the *Rancid Cat* came a clunking sound, as though a Neanderthal were beating two rocks together in an attempt to invent music. Blake shot a look at Nicki; similarly perched on the edge of her seat, she was tightening her seatbelt.

The ship tipped sideways.

Sprot, Blake thought. *Is it too late to find another ship?*

The *Rancid Cat* righted itself and not so much flew as shuddered forward, like a spider that has had its rear legs crushed by a nasty child. It looked increasingly like the ship was attempting a slow roll out of the Seven Ways dock.

'Don't you think—' Blake began.

'Leave the captaining to me!' bellowed Goyle. 'I've flown this galaxy for the better part of half a century and I'll not have landlubbers tell me how to fly my own ship!'

Another moment passed.

'Captain Goyle,' Nicki said carefully. 'We are upside down.'

'I know that, missy.'

'That's Agent Steel.'

'Missy Steel, I know that.' Goyle was pulling and pushing on a lever like someone trying to get water out of an old well. 'I'm the captain here. I know what I'm doing.'

'*He knows what he's doing! Wrrrasrrkk!*' the parrot screeched. '*He knows what he's doing!*'

A hum started from the vessel's rear. Blake wasn't sure if it was the engine warming up or building to detonation. The vessel turned until they were upright and inched out of the space dock. Something that sounded like a New Year's Eve novelty popped under the floor as a fresh stink of cabbage filled the cabin.

Blake wiped sweat from his brow. He had a vision of rendering Captain Rasmussen Goyle unconscious and locking him in his bathroom.

Just as he was convinced this was the best course of action, the ship gave a sudden surge forward and Earth slid past the front window.

'I'm setting a course for Mars,' Captain Goyle said, stabbing at buttons.

'It's the fourth planet,' Nicki said.

Goyle spun round to Blake. 'Can ye not turn her off, man!'

'Turn me off?' Nicki fumed. 'Turn me—'

'How long till we reach Mars?' Blake interrupted.

'We'll have sub-light speed in thirty seconds,' Goyle said. 'Just as long as the calipers hold out.'

'The calipers? What are the calipers?'

'Well, they control the—oh, never mind, man.' He pushed a lever forwards. 'We'll be fine as long as they don't fail.'

'And if they fail?'

'You don't want to know.'

'I *do* want to know.'

'No, you don't,' Goyle chuckled. He seemed to find the possibility of failing calipers immensely amusing. 'But try getting through life with no skin.'

'*No skin?*'

'*No skin! Aarrrrrkkk!*' The parrot laughed. '*No skin! No skin!*'

The ship gave a final shudder as the engine burped

and the Earth went out of view. A few seconds later they roared past the moon at a disturbingly close range. Blake could actually see Tycho City, and the flickering lights of the Armstrong Casino.

Then black space filled the screen.

Goyle gave them a broad smile. 'The calipers are holding fine,' he said. 'But the juniper leads are a little hot.'

'Which means?'

'My cabbage is probably burning.'

Blake kept his mouth shut, pulled out his haggis and mushrooms pills and ate one.

'Blake,' Nicki said. 'Give me one of those. It might drown out the cabbage smell.'

Chewing in silence, Blake stared through the window. A few minutes later, a red dot appeared.

Before the breakup of his marriage, Blake had travelled to many planets. Strangely, however, he had never been to Mars. And now he was about to step onto the red planet for the first time.

Centuries of terraforming had transformed it from a cold, dusty rock in space to a lively, thriving society. People had moved there in the early years of spaceflight, intent on building a new life on a new world, creating a civilisation free of the constraints of Earth.

The dot grew larger by the second.

Mars, Blake thought. *A place of dreams. Of hopes. A place of—*

Burgers?

It wasn't Mars. It was a floating restaurant, some sort of abandoned greasy diner and service station. It was shaped like an enormous saucer floating in space and the dome at its centre had a sign with a winking moustachioed man on top. The words beneath read:

Moxy's Service Stop!
If it's not Moxy, it's Poxy!

The *Rancid Cat* slowed down.

'What are you doing?' Blake asked.

'Ye wanted to catch up with Badde?' Goyle said. 'He's stopped at Moxy's.'

'What?'

Goyle pointed to a service hangar cut into the dome. 'The *Star of Fire* just pulled in there,' he said.

'Are you sure?'

'I'm Rasmussen Goyle! I once followed a ship to the middle of a black hole and back!'

'That's ridiculous,' Nicki said. 'Nothing can escape a black hole. Not even light!'

'The engines *were* running a little hot.'

'Just land this ship,' Blake snapped. 'Who knows what Badde's got planned.'

Goyle aimed for the force field protecting the service hangar from the vacuum of space. It shimmered as they entered and gravity took over. The *Rancid Cat* tipped, but Goyle brought it level, and they hit the deck in what would probably be best described as a well-conceived crash.

'There!' he said. 'Can I fly? Or can I fly?'

Nobody answered.

Blake and Nicki disembarked via the *Rancid Cat*'s exit ramp located under the ship. The landing bay was empty except for the *Star of Fire*.

'Why do you think Badde's here?' Nicki asked Blake.

'It's either engine trouble or he had to pick up something.'

'Or it's a trap.'

Drawing their blasters, Blake and Nicki cautiously approached the other ship.

'I don't see any movement,' Nicki said.

Then, from underneath the vessel, they saw Badde, with an unconscious Lisa over his shoulder, appear from behind a landing strut.

'There!' Blake yelled.

Badde disappeared through a nearby exit. Blake and Nicki followed and soon found themselves in an egg-shaped room with thousands of flashing coloured lights set into the walls. At the other end stood Badde, Lisa still over his shoulder.

'So this is what you look like in the flesh, Carter,' Badde sneered. 'I imagined you to be taller, stronger and not so ugly.'

'Put her down,' Blake said.

'I don't think so.'

'You're not going anywhere.'

'It's you who's not going anywhere,' Badde said.

He stepped out the door, taking Lisa with him. Blake and Nicki went to follow—until the room exploded with light.

34

Blake found himself standing in a street adjacent to a graveyard. Most of the gravestones had fallen over. Weeds sprouted everywhere and a rusted fence disappeared behind some monuments. Nestled among the plots was a solitary palm tree, so weighed down with dead fronds it looked ready to topple over.

But the strangest thing, thought Blake, was how everything was in shades of grey or black: the graveyard, the trees, the sky. Only he and Nicki had colour. Beyond the slice of graveyard was charcoal darkness. Dramatic music—something from an old horror film—was emanating from the gloom.

'What's going on?' Blake asked.

'I can make a guess,' Nicki said, looking around. 'I think we stepped into an old movie chamber.'

'What's a movie chamber?'

'They haven't been used for years. It's a holographic room that shows a movie, but viewers can actually be part of it.'

Blake dimly remembered them. 'Weren't those things faulty?' he asked. 'Some people even got killed in them.'

'The safety triggers were easily disengaged. That's probably why Badde led us in here. One wrong move and we're toast.'

'So this is just a simulation,' Blake said, raising his blaster. 'I can blow a hole in the wall to free us.'

Nicki gently nudged the weapon down. 'Whatever you do, don't shoot,' she said. 'The laws of space are completely warped in here. You might think you're aiming at a wall, but you're actually aiming at your own head. You might kill yourself or, even worse, me!'

Blake frowned. 'So why is everything grey?' he asked.

'This must be a really old film. Wait a minute,' Nicki said, pointing. 'Look.'

Words in a plain font appeared in mid-air before the cemetery.

'*Plan 9 from Outer Space*,' Blake read.

'Wow,' Nicki said, admiration in her voice. 'This was voted the worst movie ever made.'

'Even worse than *Attack of the Killer Slugs*?'

Zeeb says:

One would think that a movie enticingly called Attack of the Killer Slugs *would at least feature killer slugs, but sadly this was not the case. In perhaps the worst case of deception ever enacted by a producer, Caleus Rickman raised more than 100 million credits to make the movie, then absconded, with only ten per cent of the film complete.*

With most of the film still left to be shot, the responsibility fell to his second-in-charge, a man by the name of Bernard Peekle. Sadly, Bernard Peekle had never made a film, let alone one with zero budget. Fortunately, however, he came from a large family, and was able to convince his non-acting siblings, parents and cousins to be the cast.

The Peekle clan had grown up as turnip farmers, and it's fair to say that none of them had missed their vocation. With no budget and no slugs, Peekle dipped his six very cute Tylarian kittens in white paint, taped cardboard horns to their heads, and tried to pass them off as the rampaging slugs determined to destroy all in their wake.

Despite his best efforts, the result was not successful. An early screening of the movie ended with an angry mob storming the cinema and burning it to the ground.

'*Plan 9 from Outer Space* is much worse,' Nicki said.

'So why do you look so happy?'

Nicki shrugged. 'I love bad movies,' she said. 'Some movies are so bad, they're good.'

'If you say so. How do we get out of here?'

'We need to push through the film,' Nicki said. 'With any luck, I can create a resonance charge through my hands to break through to the end credits.'

She grabbed hold of the nearby palm. Jamming her fingers into the bark, she reefed the trunk apart. They pushed through into a 20th-century suburban street, leaving the opening credits and dramatic music behind.

Here the sky was brighter, but everything was still grey. Across the street, an old man had left his home.

A voice rang out from above.

'The sky to which she had once looked was now only a covering for her dead body…'

'Wow,' Nicki hissed, her face aglow. 'This is fantastic.'

'It is?'

'That's Bela Lugosi.'

'Bela what?'

'Bela Lugosi! He was the original Dracula.'

Blake stared at him. 'He *does* look like a vampire,' Blake said. 'Very pasty faced.'

'That's only partly because the film was shot in black and white,' Nicki said. 'Lugosi ended up as a morphine addict, and died before they'd finished filming. His later scenes were filmed using a double.'

The old man noticed them and made a rude gesture.

'Sorry!' Nicki yelled out.

'I've got two scenes in this lousy picture!' Lugosi yelled. 'And you decide to gatecrash one of them!' Muttering under his breath, he marched down the street.

'Let's get moving,' Blake said. 'He seems like a grouch.'

The voiceover continued:

'The old man left that home, never to return again…'

Blake and Nicki stepped into the next scene to find themselves on a dark, busy street. Cars sped past, but it was impossible to make out who was driving. A whooshing sound came from above.

'You've got to be joking,' Blake said, staring up.

Nicki laughed. 'It's a flying saucer,' she said. 'That's what people thought spaceships looked like in the 20th century.'

'Really? It looks like a saucepan lid.'

'It probably *is* a saucepan lid.'

It suddenly became very light. The scene had cut to a location outside a rundown cocktail bar. A man in a suit had just left carrying a bottle.

'Who's that?' Blake asked.

'An extra playing an old drunk. He's about to give up drinking because he sees one of the flying saucers.'

'I'd give up drinking after watching this film.'

The man peered up as the voiceover went on.

'There comes a time in each man's life when he can't even believe his own eyes.'

'It's terrible dialogue,' Blake said.

Nicki giggled. 'It's truly awful, isn't it?'

'Can we go?'

'You don't know art when you see it.'

Grabbing the wall of a nearby house, Nicki stretched a hole for them to push through.

The next scene took place back in the cemetery and it was dark again. Blake pointed at a faint light ahead.

'What is that?' he asked. 'Please tell me it's the end credits.'

'No,' Nicki said, gripping his arm with excitement. 'It's a really seminal scene! Inspector Daniel Clay has been transformed into a zombie. This is where he makes his terrifying rise from the grave.'

'Yeah. Terrifying,' Blake muttered. 'I've rarely been so scared.'

Whoever was playing Clay couldn't even climb out of the hole. Dramatic music beat through the cemetery.

'It's probably the best scene in the movie,' Nicki said.

'Other than the end credits?'

The actor playing Clay finally escaped his grave, giving Blake a better look at him.

'Wow,' he said.

'He's played by Tor Johnson,' Nicki said. 'A wrestler.'

Blake took a step back. The guy was enormous. Instant death would result if he sat on you.

'No kidding.'

The man's eyes focused on them.

'We're just passing through,' Blake said, nervously. 'Don't mind us.'

The actor/detective/zombie started towards Blake and Nicki with surprising speed. Before Blake could move, the man had lunged at him, throwing a punch. Blake ducked, but not quickly enough, and he was knocked to the ground.

As he lay stunned, Blake watched Nicki slam Clay in the face. The huge man slumped in a heap, out cold.

Then the entire room shuddered. Daniel Clay flickered out of existence as a door appeared, and Rasmussen Goyle stuck his head through.

'Are ye going to take all day?' he asked. 'Badde's got a head start!'

Blake and Nicki scrambled after him.

35

'I'd almost given up on ye!' Goyle bellowed as they took their seats at the bridge.

'We got sidetracked,' Blake snapped. 'Where's Badde?'

'He took a pot shot at our starboard engine about ten minutes back. He wrecked one of the fusion generators.'

'Which means?'

'I'm not sure we'll be able to catch him.'

The *Rancid Cat* soon veered sideways out of the landing bay. After righting the ship, Goyle punched a few buttons on the console. A tube broke loose, spurting green liquid all over the floor.

'There's me soup,' Goyle muttered.

He looked at a display, wiped some fluid from it and then shook his head.

'A generator's dead,' he announced. 'It'll take us six months to reach Mars.'

'There must be something you can do!' Blake said.

'There is a possibility,' Goyle said, shoving aside a bag of trash tied to the console with string. 'But I'd hoped never to use it.'

'Use what?' Nicki asked, giving Blake a worried glance.

'It's some ancient tech I found in a temple under a live volcano on Selarius Nine. It's half-science, half-magic and half-something else.'

'Uh,' Blake said. 'That's three halves.'

'That's how strange it is.'

'*Strange!*' the parrot shrieked.

'It's known as the Dream Glider.' Goyle flipped up a panel to reveal a transparent red dome. 'If the legend's true, when I push this button, there will be a direct connection to my brain, which will read where I want to go and transport us there instantly. Otherwise...'

'Otherwise...?' Blake said.

'You're better off not knowing.'

'I want to know.'

'All right. You've forced it out of me. There's a small chance it could compress this ship to something the size of a can of sardines.'

'*Sardines!*' the parrot shrieked, as its head spun

360 degrees. Winking at Blake, it ejected more pellets from its rear end. '*Sardines!*'

Blake swallowed. 'I wanted to lose some weight,' he said, 'but that's not what I had in mind.'

'We've got to do it,' Nicki said. 'Otherwise we'll never catch Badde.'

'You're right,' Blake said. 'Do it.'

Goyle sighed as his finger hovered over the button. 'I just hope the silicon leads are connected,' he said. 'If not, we'll blow ourselves to kingdom come.'

Before Blake could suggest checking, Goyle pushed the button. At first, the ship did nothing. Then it gave a shudder, made a hiccupping sound and vibrated—alarmingly.

'What's happening?' Blake asked.

'I think it's—'

Vroooooooom!

Blake was airborne. He crashed into the rear bulkhead with Nicki, Goyle and the parrot. The main console exploded, showering them all with debris. A half-cooked cabbage slammed Blake in the face.

'There goes me breakfast!' Goyle rasped.

Blake struggled against the g-force. He fought to push himself off the wall, but the ship was accelerating too fast for him to make any headway. One of the seats broke off and speared towards Goyle. Nicki caught it.

'Thanks, missy,' the captain grunted.

'It's Agent Steel!'

The whine of the engines lessened and Blake felt

the g-force subside as they all slid to the floor in an untidy heap. The parrot ejected more plastic pellets onto Blake's head.

'That bird doesn't like me,' he grumbled, climbing to his feet.

'His name's Columbus,' Goyle said. 'Named after an ancestor.'

They stumbled over debris to the front window.

Goyle pointed excitedly. 'Here we be!' he cried. 'Mars!'

The red planet loomed below. Two centuries ago it had been a cold, red ball in space, but now it was a mottled green and crimson sphere with water covering half its surface.

'Can you see Badde's ship?' Blake asked.

'It be on the sensors! Straight ahead!'

The *Star of Fire* appeared. It was very close to the pale blue atmosphere.

'He's preparing to jump to sub-light speed,' Goyle said.

'Can we stop him?'

'I can fire on his engines.' Goyle hit a button and a joystick appeared from the console. 'I wasn't expecting a fight, so I'll have to compromise.'

He fired on the *Star of Fire*.

They watched the projectile arrow through space.

'Captain Goyle,' Blake said. 'Is that a cabbage?'

'Necessity is the mother of invention,' Goyle said. 'Or something.'

It slammed into the rear of the other ship and they saw a brief flash. Goyle let out a triumphant cry.

'A direct hit! That's taken out their sub-light engine!' he yelled. 'They'll not be going anywhere fast.'

The ship veered towards the planet.

'He's landing to make repairs,' Nicki said. 'Maybe we can—'

Everything went dark. The console displays faded, the engines stopped and the lighting failed. It was like being in a coffin.

Even the parrot died and fell off Captain Goyle's shoulder.

'*Columbus!*'

Goyle scrambled to resuscitate the mechanical creature.

'What the sprot's going on?' Blake demanded.

'Dead!' Goyle wailed. 'Dead!'

Blake grabbed him. 'Forget the parrot!' he yelled. 'What's wrong with the ship?'

'There be nothing wrong with the ship!' Goyle shook him off. 'Some sort of pulse has wiped out all our power.'

The Super-EMP!

'Nicki!' Blake turned to her. 'Badde must have fired the—'

But Nicki was frozen. She was like a statue, stuck in the very instant of leaning forwards to speak.

'Everything electrical is fried! Destroyed!' Goyle sobbed. 'Including Columbus!'

The EMP had knocked out—maybe even destroyed—

every circuit in the ship, and Nicki as well. Blake reached over and touched her hand. Earlier she had been warm to the touch. Now she was stone cold, the bright blue spark in her eyes gone.

Blake peered through the windscreen. The *Rancid Cat* was still heading towards the planet. If they didn't turn around, they would burn up in the atmosphere.

'Captain! We've got to change direction!'

'Dead! Dead!' Goyle appeared traumatised by the death of the parrot. 'Life be not worth living without—'

Blake slapped him across the face. 'Listen! We're going to die if you don't take control of this ship!'

The words seemed to bring Goyle around. Wiping away his tears, he lurched back into the captain's chair and started stabbing controls.

'Can you restart the ship?' Blake asked.

'I can't perform miracles,' Goyle said. 'The helm won't respond, the engines are shot—'

Mars now filled the window.

'It's getting very hot in here,' Blake said.

'We're going to burn up.'

'Surely there's some way to restart the engines or adjust our descent?'

Goyle stared into the distance. 'Aye,' he muttered to himself. 'That's it.'

'What's it?'

'The manual override in the engine room can adjust the angle of the wings.'

'Which means?'

'I'll be able to manoeuvre the ship.'

'So we can land on the surface.'

'It won't be easy,' Goyle said, climbing from his seat. 'Those controls haven't been moved in years—'

Blake glanced back at Nicki. If this didn't succeed, he'd never see her again. While Goyle dragged piles of rubbish away from a hatch, Blake reached out and touched her hand again.

'Thanks,' he said. 'For everything.'

Blake went with Goyle down the hatch to a room that seemed to double as the engine room and kitchen. The air was stifling.

'We've got minutes before we burn up,' Goyle said, pointing to a crankshaft in the middle of the floor. 'You've got to pull back on the crank.'

'Me?'

'I've got to helm the ship.'

Goyle disappeared back through the hatch as Blake grabbed the control. 'How far back do I have to pull it?'

'I'll tell you when to stop,' Goyle yelled.

Blake grasped it hard and pulled. Nothing happened. He dragged back on it with all his might until he felt his face growing red.

Nothing.

'It's not moving!'

'Have ye disengaged the brake?'

Blake looked down and cursed. He pushed a lever aside.

'Try again!' Goyle yelled.

This time the crank moved begrudgingly towards Blake. Sweat ran down his face and into his eyes. The ship was shuddering and the heat intensifying. Smoke poured past the window.

'More, lad! We need another twenty degrees on the column or we're dead.'

Sprot, Blake thought. *It's now or never.*

He applied every bit of force he could to the lever. It was slippery with his sweat, but somehow he clung on. His whole body shook with effort.

'We need another fifteen degrees!' Goyle cried. 'We're burning up!'

Blake had used up every last bit of strength he had, but now he saw the control mechanism inching back towards its starting position.

'The air resistance is pushing it out of alignment,' Goyle screamed. 'We're finished! Finished!'

Blake thought of Lisa.

He applied every last iota of strength—and for the briefest of moments he was able to stop the lever from moving back into position. Then, heartbreakingly, it started to draw away from him again as smoke filled the cabin and the interior began burning up.

That's it, he thought. *I've done my best, but we're done.*

I'm sorry, Lisa.

Then a golden hand reached out of nowhere and grasped the shaft.

'Will someone turn on the air-conditioning? This heat is destroying my hair.'

'Nicki!'

She grabbed the shaft with her other hand and pulled.

'I thought you were dead!' Blake said.

'That EMP didn't do my circuitry any good,' Nicki said, as she pulled back on the shaft. 'But my human side was able to initialise my cybernetic repair protocols. I'm only operating at twenty per cent, but I'll be right as rain in a week.'

They turned their attention to the shaft. With Nicki's assistance, the lever started to pull back again.

'We need another seven degrees,' Goyle screamed. 'Come on, ye landlubbers! Pull back, blast ye!'

'I knew we should have thrown him out the airlock,' Blake muttered.

'There's still time,' Nicki said.

'Five degrees…four degrees…three…' Goyle paused. 'That's it! The wings are level! I've locked them.'

The control stick loosened in their hands.

'We're gliding,' Goyle cried. 'We've done it!'

Exhausted, Blake and Nicki made their way back to the bridge.

'So we're saved,' Blake said, grinning. 'We're going to live.'

'No,' Goyle said. 'We're still finished.'

'*What?*'

'All we've done is adjusted our angle of pitch,' Goyle

said. 'I still need power to land.' He slammed his fist on the console. 'We're as dead as a dodo.'

> *Zeeb says:*
>
> *It must be pointed out that dodos are not actually extinct. An enormous colony of them exists on Qangus Four as a result of a crashed spaceship and a love affair gone wrong. Anyway, that's another story.*

'You boys are forgetting my electrifying personality,' Nicki said, reaching behind her hair and pulling out an extension lead. 'Where do I plug in?'

A few minutes later, Goyle had the ship restarted and the engines operational—or what passed for operational. The vessel shuddered and weaved, but that may have been Goyle's usual manner of flying. The *Rancid Cat* came in to an untidy landing on the edge of a red hill.

'We've done it again,' Goyle said, patting the control panel. 'We're still the best ship this side of Qualargus Prime.'

Blake and Nicki exchanged glances.

'Don't say it,' Blake said.

'It's not worth it,' she agreed, turning to Goyle. 'Do you know where we are?'

'Robot lass, we're on Mars.'

'That's Agent Steel,' Nicki said, through clenched teeth, 'and can you be a little more precise?'

'We're very close to the bilge rat.'

'Is that a pub?' Blake asked.

'No! It's the slimy pirate you've been chasing,' Goyle explained. 'Bartholomew Badde.'

'What? Where is he?'

'His ship's about three miles east of here. There's also a building nearby, some kind of bunker.'

'Badde could be at either location,' Nicki said.

'Then we need to split up,' Blake said. 'Nicki, you go to the ship. I'll take the building. Goyle, you stay here.'

They started for the door.

'How will we stop Badde?' Nicki asked.

'I wish I knew.'

Blake breathed in deeply as he made his way up the ancient riverbed. A million years ago the ancient waters of Mars would have run freely along this channel. Now it was bone dry. On both sides, low-lying shrubbery dotted the dusty plains. A single tree sat on the horizon.

Rounding a hill, he saw the building, a rectangular concrete structure without windows, and a door at one end. Goyle had been right in describing it as a bunker. If it was a home, it was the most unhomely home Blake had ever seen.

Nearing the building, Blake climbed from the riverbed. A dam, thirty feet across, lay next to the building. Martian land was cheap, but water was precious. Blake peered at the dam. Feldspar had said the suit failed in water. If he could get Badde into the dam, he might be able to stop him.

He wondered how Nicki was faring. She would be at the *Star of Fire* by now. Blake tried raising her on his wristcomm, but got only static.

Badde's probably blocking the signal, Blake thought. *At least I've got the element of surprise.*

'Ahem.' A voice came from behind Blake. 'Are you looking for me?'

Okay, Blake thought. *Maybe I don't have the element of surprise.*

36

Badde was dressed in the phase suit. It shimmered slightly in the light of the red planet.

Blake pulled out his blaster. 'Where's my daughter?' he demanded. 'Where's Lisa?'

'She's back at my ship. No doubt your robot has already retrieved her.' Badde shrugged. 'Never mind. I'll get to them once I've finished with you.'

'You're under arrest.'

Badde laughed. 'Really?'

'Yes. For robbery, kidnapping, extortion and...' Blake tried to think of more charges. '...for being very unpleasant.'

'You can't arrest what you can't touch.'

'We'll see about that,' Blake said, pulling the trigger.

The stun blast passed harmlessly through Badde and ricocheted off the embankment behind him.

Blake turned and ran. *The dam's only twenty feet away*, he thought. *If I can reach it—*

Bang!

A shock of pain ran through Blake's left leg. He felt as though he'd been hit with a baseball bat. His leg gave way and he went sprawling, blood pouring from a wound. Badde held an old-fashioned weapon in his hand.

'It's a revolver,' Badde explained. 'A gun from ancient Earth that fires a metal projectile.' He started towards Blake.

Blake struggled to stand, but fell. He dragged himself along the ground, Badde following sedately behind.

'I'm rather pleased you survived my little diversion at Moxy's Diner,' Badde said, conversationally. 'It's more appropriate that you should die at my hands. The greatest evil genius the galaxy has ever seen should duel his nemesis to the death.'

'You are the greatest criminal the galaxy has ever known,' Blake grunted, trying to play for time. He was almost at the water. 'After all, you're responsible for the bank robbery on Tarzus Four.'

'No, I didn't do that one.'

'The jewel robbery on Sigmus Nine.'

'Uh, uh. Not me either.'

'What about the heist on Garbus Twelve?'

Badde's face brightened. 'That was me!' he said.

The cold water of the dam was almost within Blake's grasp as Badde grabbed his left leg and dragged him backwards.

Blake screamed in agony.

'Sorry,' Badde said. 'Did I hurt you?'

Blake rolled over and made a desperate grab for Badde, but his hands passed through him. It was like trying to hold on to a ghost.

'I know all about the suit's weakness,' Badde said, nodding towards the dam. 'That little problem with water. How frustrating it must be for you. Salvation being so close at hand, yet so far away.'

'You'll never get away with this,' Blake groaned.

Badde smiled. 'I already have,' he said, plunging his hand directly into the centre of Blake's chest. 'You may not be able to touch me, but I can certainly touch you.'

At first Blake felt a stinging sensation. Then it grew more painful as the strength went from his body.

'I'm going to squeeze your heart,' Badde said, 'until it pops.'

Badde picked Blake up off the ground with his hand jammed in his chest. His strength was incredible. As he dangled Blake above him like a ragdoll, the pain in Blake's chest grew ever more crushing. He tried clawing again at Badde, but there was no way to touch him.

No, Blake thought. *It can't end like this*.

Badde laughed. 'What does it feel like to die?' he asked. 'Knowing you'll never see your loved ones again?'

Blake's mind went back to Lisa and Astrid.

I've been such a fool! he thought. *I should have been a better husband! A better father to Lisa!*

Blake reached into his coat pocket.

'Your gun won't help you,' Badde laughed.

'I'm not reaching for my gun,' Blake grunted. 'I need to ask you a question.'

'What is it?'

Holding his hand up high, Blake flicked open the souvenir bottle that Lisa had given him at the Wet'n'Wild park. 'I really need to know,' Blake said. 'How deep is your love?'

He poured the bottle onto Badde. The suit flickered and sparked as Badde's eyes opened in terror.

'No!' he cried.

'Yes,' Blake said.

Blake dropped the bottle as Badde released him. The open bottle started to pass through the top of Badde's head as the phase suit failed completely. The bottle firmly jammed in his brain, the evil genius gave a soundless scream, hatred filling his eyes. He toppled dead to the ground.

Blake lay back on the red Martian soil. The pain in his chest was very bad. An eternity seemed to pass, and then—

'Dad!'

Lisa and Nicki knelt beside him.

'My heart—'

Lisa threw her arms around him. 'Dad,' she wept. 'Hold on!'

Blake gazed up at the pale blue sky. He was fading. Badde's last act had been to kill him after all. The pain was like a vice crushing his chest. 'Stay strong, old man,' Nicki said.

Blake struggled to speak. 'Listen...' he said.

'Is it Astrid?' Nicki asked. 'A message for her?'

'No...' Blake grunted. 'Can you move? You're kneeling on my arm.'

EPILOGUE

Blake Carter woke in a hospital bed to find himself surrounded.

Astrid was there, and Lisa. Nicki hovered in the corner, a worried expression on her golden face. Then Blake noticed Assistant Director Cecil Pomphrey in the chair next to the bed.

'Welcome back, Agent Carter,' Pomphrey said.

'Thanks.' Blake's eyes moved from one person to the other, trying to judge the mood. 'Am I in trouble?'

'No!' Lisa shot a look at Pomphrey. 'My dad's not in trouble. Is he?'

Pomphrey's face was dark. 'Trouble's not the word to describe it,' he said.

'Maybe heroic is a better word,' Astrid said. 'Nicki and my husband saved our daughter, stopped Earth from being destroyed by a Super-EMP and retrieved the phase suit. You should be giving them medals!'

'Look, I can't—'

'Big medals,' Astrid said firmly. 'Otherwise we go to the media, and you know what they're like.'

Blake watched resignation fill Pomphrey's face. He may have been a tough guy, but the assistant director had not dealt with the likes of Astrid Carter. He glanced at Blake, beseechingly.

'The ex-wife,' Blake said, as if that explained everything.

'We'll leave you to talk,' Astrid said. 'I know you're probably planning to catch your next evil genius, or planet eater, or whatever it is you do.'

Lisa kissed Blake's cheek. 'I love you, Dad,' she said. 'You're the best.'

It almost made everything worthwhile.

'We'll see you for dinner when you get out,' Astrid said.

'D-dinner?'

'Yes,' she said, pausing in the doorway. 'It's the meal at the end of the day when families get together.'

Blake Carter nodded dumbly, a catch in his throat. After they left, he turned to Pomphrey.

'I can explain,' Blake began. 'It was my idea. I ordered Nicki...no, threatened her to help me—'

'That's funny. She said the same thing about you.'

'Ignore her. She's out of control. Needs a reboot.'

'Thanks,' Nicki said.

'Anytime.' Blake turned to Pomphrey. 'So…what *is* going to happen?'

'Will we give you a medal?' Pomphrey asked. 'Or simply toss you in jail and throw away the key? You and Agent Steel ignored my orders to drop this case and instead broke into a government facility. Jail is probably too good for you.' He glanced at Nicki. 'No matter how long the sentence.' Sighing, he added, 'But you *were* operating under duress. A young girl *was* being held hostage.'

'And we caught Badde,' Blake added.

Nicki shook her head. 'Not quite.'

'What?'

'Oh, you nailed Badde,' Pomphrey said. 'Or the thing pretending to be him.'

'The thing…'

Pomphrey nodded in Nicki's direction. 'No offence.'

'None taken.'

'It was a robot you took out on Mars,' Pomphrey explained. 'A very sophisticated robot. We believe Badde was using it as a front for his operation.'

'So it was never really him?'

Pomphrey shook his head.

'And the real Badde?'

'Still a mystery, I'm afraid,' Cecil Pomphrey said, standing. 'Blake, you are not to return to work until you're completely recovered. Nicki, I'll expect a full report on my desk by tomorrow morning.'

'Yes, sir.'

Pomphrey hesitated at the door. 'I thought this partnership would work,' he said. 'Looks like I was right. I've got an offworld assignment for you when you're ready.'

Then he was gone.

Nicki and Blake turned to each other.

'Did we really get away with this?' Nicki asked. 'No jail time? And maybe even a medal?'

It was almost too much for Blake to take in. They weren't in jail. Lisa was safe. And Astrid was expecting him for dinner.

But Badde had escaped.

'That's unfortunate about Badde,' Nicki said.

'I never would have guessed—' Blake stared at Nicki. She was wearing a strange expression. 'What is it?'

'There's something you should know,' she said, uncomfortable. 'When they examined it…the robot…they found its components were manufactured in a particular way. Showing a particular craftsmanship, if you like.'

'So?'

'Whoever made it also made me,' Nicki said. 'I don't know what that means. Did Badde make us? Or did he employ someone else to—'

'It doesn't matter, does it?'

Nicki clenched her fists. 'It does matter!' she snapped. 'You have to know you can trust me!'

'I know I can trust you.'

'How?'

'Because you're my partner,' he said, holding out his hand.

'You're crazy,' Nicki said. 'But it's your funeral.'

They shook.

'I wonder what this special assignment is,' Blake said.

'I don't know, but it involves Venus.'

'Venus? How're we getting there?'

Nicki pushed a button on her wristcomm and a voice that Blake knew all too well sang out loud and clear.

'Ay, landlubbers!' It was Captain Rasmussen Goyle. 'They say we're flying to Venus next! Bring yer blasters! The planet's overrun with zombies and they'll eat yer face off as soon as look at yer!'

'*Zombies!*' the parrot screamed. '*Zombies!*'